# The COLOURED LANDS

## FAIRY STORIES, COMIC VERSE AND FANTASTIC PICTURES

### G. K. CHESTERTON

WITH A NEW AFTERWORD BY MARTIN GARDNER

ILLUSTRATED BY THE AUTHOR

DOVER PUBLICATIONS, INC.
MINEOLA, NEW YORK

*Bibliographical Note*

This Dover edition, first published in 2009, is a slighty altered republication of the work first published by Sheed & Ward, New York, in 1938. The color plates from the original edition have been grouped between pages 18 and 48 in this edition. The list of color illustrations on page 6 has been remade to reflect these changes.

*Library of Congress Cataloging-in-Publication Data*

Chesterton, G. K. (Gilbert Keith), 1874–1936.
   The coloured lands : fairy stories, comic verse and fantastic pictures / by G. K. Chesterton ; Illustrated by the author ; with a new afterword by Martin Gardner.
      p. cm.
   ISBN-13: 978-0-486-47115-0
   ISBN-10: 0-486-47115-2
   I. Title.

PR4453.C4C55 2009
823'.912—dc22

2008048698

Manufactured in the United States of America
Dover Publications, Inc., 31 East 2nd Street, Mineola, N.Y. 11501

*The*
# COLOURED
# LANDS

# CONTENTS

# CONTENTS

# CONTENTS

## BLACK AND WHITE ILLUSTRATIONS (*continued*)

---

Dates are shown in the above list wherever they are known. It is of interest to note that, as G. K. Chesterton was born in 1874, the earliest work included here, *Half-hours in Hades*, was written when he was seventeen and the two stories illustrated in black and white (*The Wild Goose Chase* and *The Taming of the Nightmare*) were written when he was eighteen.

Note: It is regrettable that the otherwise delightful artwork of G. K. Chesterton is marred by racial caricatures. They have been retained as intrinsic to the cultural perspectives of the author and his times.

## ACKNOWLEDGEMENTS

Acknowledgements are due to the following friends who have most kindly lent, for inclusion in this volume, drawings, stories and poems given to them by Mr. Chesterton: MRS. T. BAYLEY, MR. E. C. BENTLEY, MRS. F. L. HALFORD, MISS E. HENNELL, MISS G. MEATES, MR. & MRS. L. OLDERSHAW, MRS. SCOLLICK.

# INTRODUCTION

OF all the varied elements that go to make up the gigantic unity called G. K. Chesterton the one that matured earliest was his artistry of fantasy and the grotesque. " The dragon," he wrote at the age of sixteen, " is certainly the most cosmopolitan of impossibilities." And his admiring schoolfellows rolled the words on their tongues and murmured to one another, " This is literature." Among the members of the Junior Debating Club, founded by him at St. Paul's School, the phrase became a sort of password.

Nor was it schoolboys alone who would feel that the essay on dragons is already literature. Twenty years later, G. K. C. put some bits of coloured chalk into his pocket, strolled out on to the downs and drew the soul of a cow—" and the soul was all purple and silver, and had seven horns and the mystery that belongs to all the beasts."

I doubt if the essay of that date could be more truly called literature than could the earlier essay, although it marks obviously an immense advance in craftsmanship. But it marks something else which makes the collection in this book one of special interest to the Chestertonian.

The element of fantasy is with many writers chiefly an escape from reality. Gilbert Chesterton, from the very first, felt it rather as an extension of reality. But his sense of how closely the two were interwoven became far keener in his later work. At sixteen the dragon, that "attractive creature (who) has walked through the romances of all ages and of all nations," is a favourite companion. His themes are demons or giants or fairies. At thirty he writes, "It is one thing to describe an interview with a gorgon or a griffin, a creature who does not exist. It is another thing to discover that the rhinoceros does exist and then take pleasure in the fact that he looks as if he didn't."

One great lesson of experience is that the actual world of God's creation is too strange not to be true. But if this realisation grew more fully on Gilbert Chesterton as his mind grew, it was there from the first, and I think it is true to say that the whole of his philosophy of life is implicated in his treatment of fantasy, fairy tale and the grotesque. One of the strongest elements in this philosophy is the need for wonder and awe in face of the world of fact, and we find this element in his earliest treatment of the subject of fairy tales. In a fragment, the handwriting of which is very juvenile, after touching on the type of legend or fairy tale common to childhood in all times and all countries, he goes on, "About the beginning of the century, Hans Andersen (may his name be hallowed) published his fairy tales. Some of them, such as the Six Swans and the Travelling Companion are like beautiful imitations of the old nursery tales, but on the whole he may be said to have originated a new kind of fairy story. Instead of dealing only with dragon-slaying princes and golden-haired princesses moving in a twilight land of terrible forests and enchanted castles, he told the histories of tin soldiers and ugly ducklings, of Christmas trees and old street lamps. Instead of teaching a child to look for magic only in imaginary worlds with the assistance of charmed swords and fairy godmothers, he put it into doll's house and toy box, in the picture gallery where the landscapes might move, as they did for little Halmer, in the garden where the flowers might talk, as they did for little Gerda. That strange, beautiful idea he was so fond of suggesting, that only people who have been good can see the fairies, has recalled to many children the ever-delightful hope of seeing those individuals, and, we will hope, induced them to adopt the prescribed preliminary step."

Here can be seen those elements that made G. K. C. later criticise the Yeats conception of fairyland and claim that a " yokel " like himself knew more than the Irish poet of the realities of the fairy world, just because they were realities. Of Yeats' conception alike of life and of fantasy, Chesterton once wrote: "A mirror is a mystical thing; but it is not so wonderful as a window. . . . I wish he had lived less among mirrors repeating his mood, and more among windows breaking in on his mood. For it is the effort to relate the mood to other realities that is creation."

Chesterton lived among windows, and, looking out upon a world of realities, he saw how those realities were the roots of fruitful fantasy. " It is the sacred stubbornness of things," he wrote, " their mystery and their suggestive limits, their shape and special character, which makes all artistic thrift and thought. The adventure is not an all-transforming enchantment, it is rather the answering of a challenge; and one in which we have hardly the choice of weapons."

Here are two conditions for the play of imagination in the creation of fantasy—the relating of a mood to other realities, and an acceptance of the challenge offered to the artist by " the sacred stubbornness of things." " If, in your bold creative way," he writes in *Orthodoxy*, " you hold yourself free to draw a giraffe with a short neck, you will really find that you are not free to draw a giraffe."

But is art to be strictly limited to exact imitation of nature? Must we draw giraffes or may we still draw dragons? Can art, especially the art of fantasy, become itself really creative? What are the limits and the possibilities of creative fantasy? An elementary lesson in the art of reading Chesterton is to expect the unexpected, and this question he put and answered in what would be with most writers a surprising place—an article on a volume of War Poetry in *The New Witness* of September 6th, 1917.

In this article he analyses where revolution in the arts is right, and where it, almost automatically, goes suddenly wrong. In a black and white world a sudden splendid production of primary colours would be a magnificent achievement. The artist who came next and mixed blue and yellow creating green would " brighten and refresh the world with what is practically a new colour."

Up to this point Chesterton is on the side of the revolutionaries:

" Then we come to the third stage, which is much more subtle and very much more disputable; but in which the artistic innovators still have a quite commendable case. It is the stage at which they claim to have new experiences too curious to be common; revelations that can hardly be denounced as a palpable democratic danger, but rather as a very impalpable aristocratic privilege. This may well be represented by the next step in the mixture of tints; the step from what used to be called secondary to what used to be called tertiary colours. The artist claims that by mixing red and green he can produce a sort of russet shade, which to many may seem a mere drab or dull brown, but which is, to a finer eye, a thing combining the richness of red and the coolness of green, in a unity as unique and new as green itself. This sort of artist generally gives himself airs; but there is something to be said for him, though he seldom says it. It is true that a combination in colour may be at once unobtrusive and exquisite; but it is precisely here, I fancy, that the innovator falls into a final error. He imagines himself an inaugurator as well as an innovator; he thinks he stands at the beginning of a long process of change; whereas, as a matter of fact, he has come to the end of it. Let him take the *next* step; let him mix one exquisite mixture with another exquisite mixture, and the result will not be another and yet more exquisite mixture; it will be something like mud. It will not be all colours but no colour; a clay as hueless as some antediluvian slime out of which no life can come. . . .

"I have purposely used a crude and elementary example; but such a law of diminishing returns certainly does affect all imaginative innovation. It specially affects, for instance, that artistic adventure which may loosely be called the fantastic. There need be no limit, for example, to the mythical monsters produced by the process which made the centaur, that was made out of a man and a horse, or the griffin, that was made out of a lion and an eagle. But in this imaginative world, at any rate, it is true that mongrels do not breed. The offspring of the Missing Link and a mule, if happily married to the promising child of a Manx cat and a penguin, would not outrun centaur and griffin, it would be something lacking in all the interesting features of man and beast and bird. It would not be a wilder but a much tamer animal than its ancestors; it would not be another and more fantastic shape; but simply shapelessness. It would return to the dust, or rather to the mud, like the too complicated colour."

Looking back on a period through which he had been fighting a battle for reality in art and life, he concludes:

"Just before the war all the arts and philosophies were fading into a sort of featureless fog owing to this ceaseless multiplication of mere innovation without definition. . . . The artist has lost his original claim on our revolutionary sympathy, as well as losing many other things, such as his time, his humility and his sense of humour; but perhaps his most appalling loss is that he has lost his original realisation of the existence of red and green."

This realisation Chesterton never lost and he felt its presence in the writers whose fantasies he loved best. "In the heart of Andersen's darkest forest or most secluded garden we feel the frontiers; we hear the seas on three sides of that narrow land."[1]

In Dickens, fantasy holds the next place to humour. But just as the humour is true human laughter, so the fantasy grows in that strange eerie twilight where trees and men have alien shapes that melt and merge back into realities. The things in Dickens that are most haunting are christened by Chesterton, " Mooreeffocish " —and ' Mooreeffoc ' is only ' coffee-room ' read backwards as the child Dickens read it in the gloom and despondency of a foggy London night during his slavery at Murdstone and Grinby. Gloomy

[1] *The New Witness*, June 10th, 1915.

fantasy is truth read backwards. Cheerful fantasy is the creation of a new form wherein man, become creator, co-operates with God.

In this book we go for a holiday with Chesterton. But beware: for in such a story as " The Wild Goose Chase," or " Homesick at Home," a profound truth will suddenly take away our breath and make the world turn over. I was taught as a child to see a landscape more vividly by bending over and looking at it upside down, and this important exercise prepared me somewhat for Chesterton. Part of the fun is that he is in one sentence speaking seriously and fooling outrageously. He will never let us forget that if man made gargoyles, God made the hippopotamus.

Attacked for want of seriousness in his philosophical writings, Chesterton replied that he was deeply serious but would hate to be solemn. For a solemn man has lost something of the image of his Creator.

" No artist," he writes, " will deny a unique good in mediæval art; a power in the Gothic for fusing the grotesque with the divine. Such craftsmen found, as it were, a special clay that could be moulded in one piece into angels and apes. I do not say that ancient stoics or modern sceptics have been unable to smile or to be serious. I do not say that the Praying Boy is not praying; or that no dignity belonged to that stone on which was written *Deo erexit Voltaire*. I say that those Greek and Gallic stones were not graven like the Gothic stones; had not that special spiritual energy and even gaiety that can be seen in any worn old waterspout sticking from the roof of Lincoln or Beauvais. For the gargoyle is really typical of the mystical utilitarianism of the Gothic; of something which got poetic good out of a gutter, and turned a vision of mere vomiting into a thing of beauty. Similarly, I do not say that pagan and secular gaiety are not as beautiful; but I do say that they are not as gay. St. Peter in a mediæval carving may be represented with a cock that is comic and meant wholeheartedly and simply to be comic; while his namesake Pierrot in the Arcadia of the age of Watteau, is something at once frivolous and sad. For Peter went out and wept bitterly; but he did not weep as bitterly as Pierrot can laugh."[1]

In telling the story of Chesterton's life and of his writings, much must be said that will strike a deeper note. But it is fitting to salute him first as a maker of fantasy which at once hid and revealed truth. As a boy there was about his fantasy a touch of solemnity, for he was an agnostic. But when he had discovered the ancient truth that is ever new, he became gay for he had found " the beginning of something bolder than military obedience and freer than civil freedom. It is a great beginning like that of a great bridge, soaring like a bird yet bearing men onward like a street; the miracle and paradox of something at once solid and in the air."[2]

MAISIE WARD.

[1] *The New Witness*, June 14th, 1918.    [2] Ibid.

# THE COLOURED LANDS

ONCE upon a time there was a little boy whose name was Tommy. As a matter of fact his name was Tobias Theodore; the former because it was an old name in the family, and the latter because it was an entirely new name in the neighbourhood. It is to be hoped that the parents who called him Tobias Theodore, moved by a natural desire to keep it quiet, agreed to call him Tommy; and anyhow we will agree to call him Tommy. It is always assumed in stories that Tommy is a common name for a boy; just as it is always assumed that Tomkins is a common name for a man. I do not really know very many boys named Tommy. I do not know any man named Tomkins. Do you? Does anybody? But this enquiry would lead us far.

Anyhow Tommy was sitting one very hot afternoon on a green lawn outside the cottage that his father and mother had taken in the country. The cottage had a bare white-washed wall; and at that moment it seemed to Tommy very bare. The summer sky was of a blank blue, which at that moment seemed to him very blank. The dull yellow thatch looked very dull and rather dusty; and the row of flower-pots in front of him, with red flowers in them, looked irritatingly straight, so that he wanted to knock some of them over like ninepins. Even the grass around him moved him only to pluck it up in a vicious way; almost as if he were wicked enough to wish it was his sister's hair. Only he had no sister; and indeed no brothers. He was an only child and at that moment rather a lonely child, which is not necessarily

A BLUE DEVIL

the same thing. For Tommy, on that hot and empty afternoon, was in that state of mind in which grown-up people go away and write books about their view of the whole world, and stories about what it is like to be married, and plays about the important problems of modern times. Tommy, being only ten years old, was not able to do harm on this large and handsome scale. So he continued to pull out the grass like the green hair of an imaginary and irritating sister, when he was surprised to hear a stir and a step behind him, on the side of the garden far away from the garden gate.

He saw walking towards him a rather strange-looking young man wearing blue spectacles. He was clad in a suit of such very light grey that it looked almost white in the strong sunlight; and he had long loose hair of such very light or faint yellow that the hair might almost have been white as well as the clothes. He had a large limp straw hat to shade him from the sun; and, presumably for the same purpose, he flourished in his left hand a Japanese parasol of a bright peacock green. Tommy had no idea of how he had come onto that side of the garden; but it appeared most probable that he had jumped over the hedge.

All that he said was, with the most casual and familiar accent, " Got the blues? "

Tommy did not answer and perhaps did not understand; but the strange young man proceeded with great composure to take off his blue spectacles.

" Blue spectacles are a queer cure for the blues," he said cheerfully. " But you just look through these for a minute."

Tommy was moved to a mild curiosity and peered through the glasses; there certainly was something weird and quaint about the discoloration of everything; the red roses black and the white wall blue, and the grass a bluish green like the plumes of a peacock.

"Looks like a new world, doesn't it?" said the stranger. "Wouldn't you like to go wandering in a blue world once in a blue moon?"

"Yes," said Tommy and put the spectacles down with a rather puzzled air. Then his expression changed to surprise; for the extraordinary young man had put on another pair of spectacles, and this time they were red.

"Try these," he said affably. "These, I suppose, are revolutionary glasses. Some people call it looking through rose-coloured spectacles. Others call it seeing red."

Tommy tried the spectacles, and was quite startled by the effect; it looked as if the whole world were on fire. The sky was of a glowing or rather glaring purple, and the roses were not so much red as red-hot. He took off the glasses almost in alarm, only to note that the young man's immovable countenance was now adorned with yellow spectacles. By the time that these had been followed by green spectacles, Tommy thought he had been looking at four totally different landscapes.

"And so," said the young man, "you would like to travel in a country of your favourite colour. I did it once myself."

Tommy was staring up at him with round eyes.

"Who are you?" he asked suddenly.

"I'm not sure," replied the other. "I rather think I am your long-lost brother."

"But I haven't got a brother," objected Tommy.

"It only shows how very long-lost I was," replied his remarkable relative. "But I assure you that, before they managed to long-lose me, I used to live in this house myself."

"When you were a little boy like me?" asked Tommy with some reviving interest.

"Yes," said the stranger gravely. "When I was a little boy and very like you. I also used to sit on the grass and wonder what to do with myself. I also got tired of the blank white wall. I also got tired even of the beautiful blue sky. I also thought the thatch was just thatch and wished the roses did not stand in a row."

"Why, how do you know I felt like that?" asked the little boy, who was rather frightened.

"Why, because I felt like that myself," said the other with a smile.

Then after a pause he went on.

"And I also thought that everything might look different if the colours were different; if I could wander about on blue roads between blue fields and go on wandering till all was blue. And a Wizard who was a friend of mine actually granted my wish; and I found myself walking in forests of great blue flowers like gigantic lupins and larkspurs, with only glimpses now and then of pale blue skies over a dark blue sea. The trees were inhabited by blue jays and bright blue kingfishers. Unfortunately they were also inhabited by blue baboons."

"Were there any people in that country?" enquired Tommy.

The traveller paused to reflect for a moment; then he nodded and said:

"Yes; but of course wherever there are people there are troubles. You couldn't expect all the people in the Blue Country to get on with each other very well. Naturally there was a crack regiment called the Prussian Blues. Unfortunately there was also a very energetic semi-naval brigade called French Ultramarines.

A BLUE-STOCKING

You can imagine the consequence." He paused again for a moment and then said: " I met one person who made rather an impression on me. I came upon him in a place of great gardens shaped in a crescent like the moon, and in the centre above a fringe of blue-gum trees there rose a great blue lustrous dome, like the Mosque of Omar. And I heard a great and terrible voice that seemed to toss the trees to and fro; and there came out between them a tremendously tall man, with a crown of huge sapphires round his turban; and his beard was quite blue. I need not explain that he was Bluebeard."

" You must have been frightened," said the little boy.

" At first perhaps," replied the stranger, " but I came to the conclusion that Bluebeard is not so black—or perhaps so blue—as he is painted. I had a little confidential talk with him, and really there was something to be said on his side of the case. Living where he did, he naturally married wives who were all blue-stockings."

" What are blue-stockings? " asked Tommy.

" Naturally you don't know," replied the other. " If you did, you would sympathise more with Bluebeard. They were ladies who were always reading books. They even read them aloud."

" What sort of books were they? "

" Blue-books, of course," replied the traveller. " They are the only kind of book allowed there. That is why I decided to leave. With the assistance of my friend the Wizard I obtained a passport to cross the frontier, which was a very vague and shadowy one, like the fine shade between two tints of the rainbow. I only felt that I was passing over peacock-coloured seas and meadows and the world was growing greener and greener till I knew I was in a Green Country. You would think that was more restful, and so it was, up to a point. The point was when I met the celebrated Green Man, who has given his name for so many excellent public houses. And then there is always a certain amount of limitation in the work and trade of these beautiful harmonious landscapes. Have you ever lived in a country where all the people were green-grocers? I think not. After all, I asked myself, why should all grocers be green? I felt myself longing to look at a yellow grocer. I saw rise up before me the glowing image of a red grocer. It was just about this time that I floated insensibly into the Yellow Country; but I did not stay there very long. At first it was very splendid; a radiant scene of sunflowers and golden crowns; but I soon found it was almost entirely filled with Yellow Fever and the Yellow Press discussing the Yellow Peril. Of the three I preferred the Yellow Fever; but I could not get any real peace or happiness even out of that. So I faded through an orange haze until I came to the Red Country, and it was there that I really found out the truth of the matter."

"What did you find out?" asked Tommy, who was beginning to listen much more attentively.

"You may have heard," said the young man, "a very vulgar expression about painting the town red. It is more probable that you have heard the same thought put in a more refined form by a very scholarly poet who wrote about a rose-red city, half as old as time. Well, do you know, it is a curious fact that in a rose-red city you cannot really see any roses. Everything is a great deal too red. Your eyes are tired until it might just as well all be brown. After I had been walking for ten minutes on scarlet grass under a scarlet sky and scarlet trees, I called out in a loud voice, 'Oh, this is all a mistake.' And the moment I had said

THE GREEN MAN

A GREEN-GROCER

that the whole red vision vanished; and I found myself standing in quite a different sort of place; and opposite me was my old friend the Wizard, whose face and long rolling beard were all one sort of colourless colour like ivory, but his eyes of a colourless blinding brilliance like diamonds.

"'Well,' he said, 'you don't seem very easy to please. If you can't put up with any of these countries, or any of these colours, you shall jolly well make a country of your own.'

"And then I looked round me at the place to which he had brought me; and a very curious place it was. It lay in great ranges of mountains, in layers of different colours; and it looked something like sunset clouds turned solid and something like those maps that mark geological soils, grown gigantic. And all along the terraces of the hills they were trenched and hollowed into great quarries; and I think I understood without being told that this was the great original place from which all the colours came, like the paint-box of creation. But the most curious thing of all was that right in front of me there was a huge chasm in the hills that opened into sheer blank daylight. At least sometimes I thought it was a blank and sometimes a sort of wall made of frozen light or air and sometimes a sort of tank or tower of clear water; but anyhow the curious thing about it was that if you splashed some of the coloured earths upon it, they remained where you had thrown them, as a bird hangs in the air. And there the Wizard told me, rather impatiently, to make what sort of world I liked for myself, for he was sick of my grumbling at everything.

"So I set to work very carefully; first blocking in a great deal of blue, because I thought it would throw up a sort of square of white in the middle; and then I thought a fringe of a sort of dead gold would look well along the top of the white; and I spilt some green at the bottom of it. As for red, I had already found out the secret about red. You have to have a very little of it to make a lot of it. So I just made a row of little blobs of bright red on the white just above the green; and as I went on working at the details, I slowly discovered what I was doing; which is what very few people ever discover in this world. I found I had put back, bit by bit, the whole of that picture over there in front of us. I had made that white cottage with the thatch and that summer sky behind it and that green lawn below; and the row of the red flowers just as you see them now. That is how they come to be there. I thought you might be interested to know it."

And with that he turned so sharply that Tommy had not time to turn and see him jump over the hedge; for Tommy remained staring at the cottage, with a new look in his eyes.

# THE DISADVANTAGE OF HAVING —
## TWO HEADS.
### A STORY —

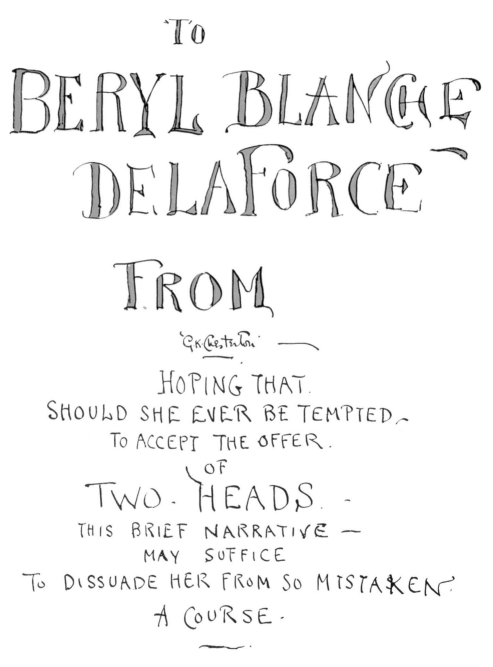

TO
BERYL BLANCHE
DE LA FORCE
FROM
'G.K.Chesterton'
HOPING THAT.
SHOULD SHE EVER BE TEMPTED.
TO ACCEPT THE OFFER.
OF
TWO. HEADS. -
THIS BRIEF NARRATIVE —
MAY SUFFICE
TO DISSUADE HER FROM SO MISTAKEN
A COURSE.

A little boy once looked over the garden fence and saw four knights with enormous crests riding by. As he is now married to a princess and moves in rather good society, he has desired me not to mention his name: so we will call him Redlegs. Being interested in such things he climbed over the fence

and ran after the knights to see where they were going. They came to a

# VERY OLD MAN.

Who was sitting on the very sharp point of a Rock, balancing himself.
The Knights, seeing by his sugar-loaf hat white beard that he was a
Magician, asked him where they could find the Princess Japonica (for
so the Princess, who is a relative of mine & desires to be ~~thus~~ described).
"The Princess Japonica" replied the Magician "lives in the Castle beyond
the Last Wood in the World, in the place where it is always sunset. She cannot
come and visit anyone and noone can visit her because there are only two
roads to it: and the right hand road is held by a Giant with one Head, and
the left hand road by a Giant with Two Heads." Then the first Knight said
with great excitement (he was Bromley-Smunk on the mother's side and
you know what they are) "I will soon clear the giant out of the way. But I
think I will confine myself to the Giant with one head. For I am a
humane man & desire to ~~do~~ cut off as few heads as possible".

So the first Knight set out along the road to the One-headed Giant. And a little while after the second set out & then the third & then the fourth, all the same way. The little boy stopped behind and talked to the Magician about the Fiscal Question. Scarcely had they dismissed this brief topic, than they saw a sad string of people coming along the road

from the One-Eyed Giant. They were the four Knights & I am sorry to say they were rather

# SMASHED.

Then the Redlegs said suddenly "I should very much like to see a Two-Headed Giant. Lend me a sword". Then they all roared with laughter and told him how silly he was to think that he could kill the Two-Headed Giant when they couldn't kill even the One-Headed Giant. But he went off all the same, with his head in the air & he found the Two-Headed Giant on the great hills where it is always Sunset. And then he found out a funny thing The Two-Headed Giant did not rush at him and tear him to pieces as he had expected. It did certainly scream & shout

and bellow and blare and with its two heads, together. But the two heads, were, as a matter of fact, screaming and shouting & bellowing and blaring in an odd way. They were screaming and shouting and bellowing & blaring at

# EACH OTHER

One head said "You are a Pro-Boer"; the other said, with bitter
humour "You're another"; in fact the argument might have gone on
for ever, growing more savage & brilliant every moment, but it was
cut short by Redlegs, who took out the great sword he had borrowed
from one of the Knights & poked it sharply into the Giant & killed him.
The huge creature sprawled & writhed like a continent in an earthquake;
and one wild head lifted itself for a moment in death & said to the
other "You are beneath my notice". Then it died happy. Redlegs went

on along the road that had been guarded by the Two-Headed Giant, until he came to the Castle of the Princess. After a few words of explanation, I need hardly say they were

# MARRIED.

—and lived happily ever afterwards. The Magician, who gave the bride away, said after the conclusion of the ceremony the following Cabalistic and totally unintelligible words. "My son, the Giant who had one head was stronger than the Giant who had two. When you grow up there will come to you other magicians who will say "Γνῶθι σέαυτον. Examine your soul, wretched kid. Cultivate a sense of the differentiations possible in a single psychology. Have nineteen religions suitable to different moods". My son, these will be wicked magicians; they will want to turn you into a two headed Giant." Redleps did not know what this meant and nor do I.

The Rose-Coloured Spectacles

# PICTURES FROM THE PAINT-BOX

# PICTURES FROM THE PAINTBOX. I.
## PRUSSIAN BLUE.

PICTURES FROM THE PAINTBOX. 2.
FRENCH
ULTRA
MARING.

PICTURES FROM THE PAINT·BOX.
3. CHINESE WHITE.

PICTURES FROM THE PAINT BOX.

4. BURNT SIENA.

45

PICTURES FROM THE PAINT-BOX. 5. IVORY ▮▮▮
BLACK

47

G.K.C'S DRAWING OF HIMSELF WHILE STILL
AT THE SLADE SCHOOL (AGED ABOUT 20)

49

# BOB-UP-AND-DOWN

IRRESPONSIBLE outbreak of one who, having completed a book of enormous length on the Poet Chaucer, feels himself freed from all bonds of intellectual self-respect and proposes to do no work for an indefinite period.

"Wot ye not wher ther start a litel town,
  Which that icleped is Bob-up-an-down."

THE CANTERBURY TALES.

They babble on of Babylon,
They tire me out with Tyre,
And Sidon putting side on,
I do not much admire.
But the little town Bob-up-and-Down,
That lies beyond the Blee,
Along the road our fathers rode,
O that's the road for me.

In dome and spire and cupola
It bubbles up and swells
For the company that canter
To the Canterbury Bells.
But when the Land Surveyors come
With maps and books to write,
The little town Bob-up-and-Down
It bobs down out of sight.

# BOB-UP-AND-DOWN

I cannot live in Liverpool,
O lead me not to Leeds,
I'm not a Man in Manchester,
Though men be cheap as weeds:
But the little town Bob-up-and-Down,
That bobs towards the sea,
And knew its name when Chaucer came,
O that's the town for me.

I'll go and eat my Christmas meat
In that resurgent town,
And pledge to fame our Father's name
Till the sky bobs up and down;
And join in sport of every sort
That's played beside the Blee,
Bob-Apple in Bob-up-and-Down,
O that's the game for me.

Now Huddersfield is Shuddersfield,
And Hull is nearly Hell,
Where a Daisy would go crazy
Or a Canterbury Bell,
The little town Bob-up-and-Down
Alone is fair and free,
For it can't be found above the ground,
O that's the place for me.

JOB PLAYING PATIENCE

# THE WHALE'S WOOING

A NEWSPAPER famous for its urgency about practical and pressing affairs recently filled a large part of its space with the headline, "Do Whales Have Two Wives?" There was a second headline saying that Science was about to investigate the matter in a highly exact and scientific fashion. And indeed it may be hoped that science is more exact than journalism. One peculiarity of that sentence is that it really says almost the opposite of what it is intended to say. We might suppose that, before printing a short phrase in large letters, a man might at least look at it to see whether it said what he meant. But behind all this hustle there is not only carelessness but a great weariness. Strictly speaking, the phrase, "Do Whales Have Two Wives?" could only mean, if it meant anything, "Do all the whales, in their collective capacity, have only two wives between them?" But the journalist did not mean to suggest this extreme practice of polyandry. He only meant to ask whether the individual whale can be reproached with the practice of bigamy. At first sight there is something rather quaint and alluring about the notion of watching a whale to see whether he lives a double life. A whale scarcely seems designed for secrecy or for shy and furtive flirtation. The thought of a whale assuming various disguises, designed to make him inconspicuous among other fishes, puts rather a strain on the imagination. He would have to keep his two establishments, one at the North Pole and the other at the South, if his two wives were likely to be jealous of each other;

53

and if he really wished to avoid becoming a bone (or whale-bone) of contention. In truth the most frivolous philanderer would hardly wish to conduct his frivolities on quite so large a scale; and the loves of the whales may well appear a theme for a bolder pen than any that has yet traced the tremendous epic of the loves of the giants.

But we have a sort of fancy or faint suspicion about where it may end. Science, or what journalism calls Science, is always up to its little games; and this might possibly be one of them. We know how some people perpetually preach to us that there is no morality in nature and therefore nothing natural in morality. We know we have been told to learn everything from the herd instinct or the law of the jungle; to learn our manners from a monkey-house and our morals from a dog-fight. May we not find a model in a far more impressive and serene animal? Shall we not be told that Leviathan refuses to put forth his nose to the hook of monogamy, and laughs at the shaking of the chivalric spear? To the supine and superstitious person, who has lingered with one wife for a whole lifetime, will not the rebuke be uttered in the ancient words; " Go to the whale, thou sluggard." Contemplating the cetaceous experiments in polygamy, will not the moralist exclaim once more: " How doth the little busy whale improve the shining hour !" Will not the way of this superior mammal be a new argument for the cult of the new Cupid; the sort of Cupid who likes to have two strings to his bow? For we are bound to regard the monster as a moral superior, according to the current moral judgments. We are perpetually told that the human being is small, that even the earth itself is small, compared with the splendid size of the solar system. If we are to surrender to the size of the world, why not to the size of the whale? If we are to bow down before planets which are larger than our own, why not before animals that are larger than ourselves? Why not, with a yet more graceful bow, yield the *pas* (if the phrase be sufficiently aquatic) to the great mountain of blubber? In many ways he looks very like the highest moral ideal of our time.

# BALLADE OF KINDNESS TO MOTORISTS

O Motorists, Motorists, run away and play,
I pardon you.   Such exercise resigned,
When would a statesman see the woods in May?
How could a banker woo the western wind?
When you have knocked a dog down I have pined,
When you have kicked the dust up I have sneezed,
These things come from your absence—well, of Mind—
But when you get a puncture I am pleased.

I love to see you sweating there all day
About some beastly hole you cannot find;
While your poor tenants pass you in a dray,
Or your sad clerks bike by you at a grind,
I am not really cruel or unkind;
I would not wish you mortally diseased,
Or deaf or dumb or dead or mad or blind,
But when you get a puncture I am pleased.

What slave that dare not smile when chairs give way?
When smart boots slip, having been lately shined?
When curates cannon with the coffee tray?
When trolleys take policemen from behind?
When kings come forth in public, having dined,
And palace steps are just a trifle greased?—
The joke may not be morbidly refined,
But when you get a puncture I am pleased.

# BALLADE OF KINDNESS TO MOTORISTS

Prince of the Car of Progress Undefined,
On to your far Perfections unappeased!
Leave your dead past with its dead children lined;
But when you get a puncture I am pleased.

LITTLE BO-PEEP

# THE JAZZ

*A Study of Modern Dancing, in the manner of Modern Poetry.*

TLANNGERSHSHSH !
Thrills of vibrant discord,
　Like the shivering of glass;
Some people dislike it; but I do not dislike it.
　I think it is fun,
Approximating to the fun
Of merely smashing a window;
But I am told that it proceeds
　From a musical instrument,
Or at any rate
　From an instrument.

Black flashes . . .
　. . . Flashes of intermittent darkness;
Somebody seems to be playing with the electric light;
　Some may possibly believe that modern dancing
Looks best in the dark.

　I do not agree with them.
I have heard that modern dancing is barbaric,
　Pagan, shameless, shocking, abominable.
No such luck—I mean no such thing.
　The dancers are singularly respectable

# THE JAZZ

To the point of rigidity,
With something of the rotatory perseverance
    Of a monkey on a stick;
But there is more stick than monkey,
    And not, as slanderers assert,
More monkey than stick.


Let us be moderate,
There are a lot of jolly people doing it,
    (Whatever it is),
Patches of joyful colour shift sharply,
    Like a kaleidoscope.
Green and gold and purple and splashes of splendid black,
    Familiar faces and unfamiliar clothes;
I see a nice-looking girl, a neighbour of mine, dancing.
    After all,
She is not very different;


She looks nearly as pretty as when she is not dancing . . .
    . . . I see certain others, less known to me, also dancing.
They do not look very much uglier
    Than when they are sitting still.


(Bound, O Terpsichore, upon the mountains,
    With all your nymphs upon the mountains,
And Salome that held the heart of a king
    And the head of a prophet;
For to the height of this tribute
    Your Art has come.)

# THE JAZZ

If I were writing an essay
—And you can put chunks of any number of essays
   Into this sort of poem—
I should say there was a slight disproportion
   Between the music and the dancing;
For only the musician dances
   With excitement,
While the dancers remain cold
   And relatively motionless
(Orpheus of the Lyre of Life
   Leading the forests in fantastic capers;
Here is your Art eclipsed and reversed,
   For I see men as trees walking).

If Mr. King stood on his head,
Or Mr. Simon butted Mr. Gray
   In the waistcoat,
Or the two Burnett-Browns
Strangled each other in their coat-tails,
   There would then be a serene harmony,
     A calm unity and oneness
   In the two arts.
   But Mr. King remains on his feet,
And the coat-tails of Mr. Burnett-Brown
   Continue in their customary position.

And something else was running in my head—
—Songs I had heard earlier in the evening;
   Songs of true lovers and tavern friends,
     Decent drunkenness with a chorus,

And the laughter of men who could riot.
And something stirred in me;
   A tradition
Strayed from an older time,
   And from the freedom of my fathers:
That when there is banging, yelling and smashing to be done,
     I like to do it myself,
   And not delegate it to a slave,
     However accomplished.
And that I should sympathise,
     As with a revolt of human dignity,
If the musician had suddenly stopped playing,
And had merely quoted the last line
Of a song sung by Mrs. Harcourt Williams:
   " If you want any more, you must sing it yourselves."

# Half Hours in Hades.

## An Elementary Handbook of Demonology.

# HALF-HOURS IN HADES

## An Elementary Handbook of Demonology

### PREFACE

IN the autumn of 1890, I was leaving the Casino at Monte Carlo in company with an eminent Divine, whose name, for obvious reasons, I suppress. We were engaged in an interesting discussion on the subject of Demons, he contending that they were an unnecessary, not to say prejudicial, element in our civilisation, an opinion which, needless to say, I strongly opposed. Having at length been so fortunate as to convince him of his error, I proceeded to furnish him with various instances in which Demons have proved beneficial to mankind, and at length he exclaimed, " My dear fellow, why do you not write a book about——" Here he coughed. The idea took so strong a hold upon me, that from that time I have taken more careful note of the habits and appearance of such specimens as come in my way, and my studies have resulted in the production of this little work, which will, I trust, prove not uninteresting to the youthful seeker after knowledge.

In my capacity as Professor of Supernatural Science at Oxford University, it has often been my duty to call upon an individual who probably knows more about all branches of the subject with which I am about to deal than any man on earth, although no one has yet persuaded him to give his knowledge to the world; and with his permission I have dedicated these pictures to him, as some slight recognition of the wisdom and experience which he has brought to my assistance in the compiling of this modest treatise.

*Baron's Court House, London.*
  *October,* 1891.

To that mature personage, the cimmerian nature of whose aspect is popularly supposed to be greatly overrated, this volume is affectionately dedicated.

# HALF-HOURS IN HADES

## CHAPTER I

### THE FIVE PRIMARY TYPES

Is it not wonderful that so few persons should know anything about the habits and appearance of those whose names are so often on their lips, and who exert so great an influence over all our lives? For those who love the study of Demonology (and I pity the man or woman who does not) it possesses an interest which will remain after health, youth and even life have departed.

It is not my intention in this simple little work to puzzle the young student with any of those dark technicalities of the Science which are only intelligible to such as have studied it for some time. I merely try to put before him, in language as simple as possible,

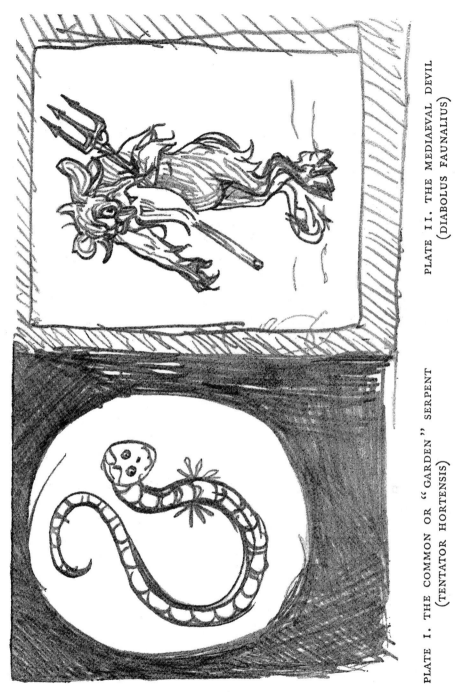

PLATE II. THE MEDIAEVAL DEVIL
(DIABOLUS FAUNALIUS)

PLATE I. THE COMMON OR " GARDEN " SERPENT
(TENTATOR HORTENSIS)

69

the various species of Demon with which he is most likely to meet, and to explain the organism of any he may have already encountered.

To proceed at once to business, I will first introduce to my young readers the Common, or "Garden" serpent, so-called because its first appearance in the world took place in a Garden. Since that time its proportions have dwindled considerably, but its influence and power have largely increased; it is found in almost everything.

The prejudice entertained by clergymen and others against this insect is most unreasonable and cruel. Were it not for the creature they destroy, their occupation would be gone, like Othello's. Yet they do all they can to stamp out and crush down this little creature, wherever he may show his hoof.

The next in importance of the specimens of this interesting branch of science is the Mediaeval Demon, whose horns, tail and claws form a remarkable contrast to the serpentine formation of our first type. So wide is the divergence between the two that many modern authorities on the subject put it in an entirely different class to the Common or Garden species, connecting it with an extinct animal of similar formation known as the Faun or Pan, which found its home in many parts of Arcadia. Be this as it may, the Mediaeval Demon is, of all the species, perhaps the one with which we are most familiar; in fact so accustomed are we to the traits and appearance of this remarkable creature that we have more or less taken it under our patronage. It is in a domesticated state the subject rather of playfulness and household merriment than of abhorrence, while the far cleverer and more graceful serpent is the object of a cruel and unreasoning persecution. But useful as the mediaeval species is found at the present day as a general source of amusement, it has of late somewhat failed to stir public interest, which is turned towards newer and more elegant varieties: some of which we shall pass briefly in review. Mr. J. Milton, in his interesting and valuable work on this subject, has discussed at some length the leading characteristics of a fine species of which

FIG. A.  DIABOLUS PARADISI PERDITI

71

FIG. B. THE RED DEVIL
(DIABOLUS MEPHISTOPHILES)

he was primarily the discoverer, and of which Fig. A. is a sketch. This magnificent animal measures at least four roods, and when floating full length on the warm gulf, of which it is an inhabitant, has been compared by its discoverer to a whale.[1]

According to Mr. Milton's theory, this animal is practically identical with the creature represented in Plate I, but, however ably supported, his view has been abandoned by most later authorities. This species is an inhabitant of warm latitudes like most of its kind, being originally found in the burning lakes and dark wildernesses of the most remote parts of the world. Its colour is, generally speaking, dark, but, like most of these creatures, this peculiarity has been much overrated, and Mr. Milton has justly pointed out the "faded

[1] See *Paradise Lost.* Book I.

splendour wan " which imparts a lighter shade to many parts of its exterior.

We now come to the discussion of a very remarkable species which are vulgarly known for the most part by their colour.

The Red Devil (Diabolus Mephistopheles) was discovered by that learned and enterprising German naturalist, Mr. Wolfgang von Goethe, who has published an interesting story of a specimen kept in a domesticated state in the house of his learned fellow-countryman, Dr. Faust. In a domestic state this creature is playful and active, but mischievous and impossible to trust. The learned doctor found it a useful and entertaining companion for many years, but was finally persuaded to part with it, on which it sought the seclusion of its native surroundings. Its colour, as suggested by its name, is, with the exception of its face and hands, a uniform red. Its height is about six feet.

Very different in appearance, yet possessed of one or two of the same habits, is the Blue Devil (Caeruleus Lugubrius). These creatures are gregarious, being usually seen and spoken of in the plural. Though formed by Super-Nature in their habits and exterior apparently for the filling of waste moors, mountains, churchyards and other obsolete places, these animals, like the Red Devil, have frequently been domesticated in rich and distinguished houses, and many of the wealthiest aristocrats and most successful men of commerce may be seen with a string of these blue creatures led by a leash in the street or seated round him in a ring on his own fireside. The noise made by this creature is singularly melancholy and depressing, and its general appearance is far from lively. But though less agile and intelligent than the Red Devil, the sobriety of its habits and demeanour have made it a suitable pet for the houses of clergymen and other respectable persons. To such an

THE BLUE DEVIL
(CAERULEUS LUGUBRIUS)

extent indeed has this domestication of the Blue Devil been carried, that many persons have denied its connection with the great class we are discussing. There can, however, be no doubt about its origin.

# Chapter II

### THE EVOLUTION OF DEMONS

On what perhaps is the most intricate and interesting part of Demonology it is impossible to say much in a work of small size and pretensions. It is unnecessary to go through the elaborate

INSTANCES OF EVOLUTION I

INSTANCES OF EVOLUTION II

76

INSTANCES OF EVOLUTION III

proof given by Mr. Darwin and transfer it to the supernatural world, but only to make a few remarks on some of the most interesting examples of diabolical evolution. When the young student grows older he will meet with others in his own experience.

INSTANCES OF EVOLUTION IV

## Chapter III

" But, mamma, can we all see devils? "

" Certainly, Charlotte, if we will take the trouble. They are constantly in our path and it is only the lazy and careless that pass them by. The human race might well learn a lesson from these little creatures, and in fact it not infrequently does. Harry here will tell you that only this morning he found a most interesting specimen while coming from church, and how pleased I was that he should have been so diligent. We can all see the common varieties in any country walk, or even in the city, where they are occasionally found, but at the same time it is to be remembered that we cannot expect to see *all* this great field of interest in this life. Dr. Brown, the vicar, who knows more about these things than you or I, children, will, I am sure, take great pleasure in some day showing you over his collection, where you will see some very rare species, not to be found in everyday life, and which are the fruits of a long career of diligent research. He possesses, I believe, the only known variety of the Pelagian ever seen in this country and will be pleased to show it you and make it vainly talk. The Boasting Anabaptist (Anabaptiste Falsegloriator) has also its representatives in his collection and he is the author of many clever works on the subject."

" But, mamma, does Dr. Brown love his little pets ? "

" I have reason to believe that he is fondly attached to them. They are never out of his sight and he has often said that he has gleaned many useful lessons from their habits. In fact he says that he would not be the man he is but for them, and one glance at Dr. Brown will make it clear that this is no exaggeration."

" Mamma, dear, do you remember what Cousin George found when he was staying with us last summer ? "

" I recollect it extremely well, Albert, and I am glad indeed to find that your memory is as vivid as mine. It had always been my belief that Cousin George would alight upon some such discovery, for I well know him as a keen observer of Supernature and I hope, my children, that you may ever be as clever Demonologists as he. I remember even as a little boy he would be always found in the haunts of these creatures among which he may almost be said to have been brought up. I predict a great future for Cousin George."

" And, mamma dear, remember that you promised to show us some experiments this evening."

" Well, children, you shall have some. Will you turn out the gas, Albert? while you Jane, will ask cook to lend us the large kettle. Harry will fetch the long wand from its place in the umbrella stand. Thank you, that is right. Now, children, for our first experiment I have here the eye of the common newt or eft, the left toe of the edible frog, the jaw of one of the blue sharks, a portion of the root of the hemlock plant, which I took no little trouble to dig up quite late last night, the liver of a blaspheming Jew, and other interesting specimens: round about the cauldron go, children, in the poisoned entrails throw. That is right. Now we will see what happens——Ah, I thought so. Do you see those two round green orbs of light, Jane? Those are the eyes of a very

interesting species, and its form will soon become apparent to us. Do not scream, Charlotte, for that would be naughty, and would perhaps frighten the little creatures, as they are very timid. By this time, children, you may perceive the outline of an attenuated figure, resembling in some respects that of a skeleton, though the ears, which you can now see moving, show that this is not the case. Lift little Harry up, James, since he is too small to see over the edge of the cauldron."

IMMORTAL IDIOTS — I.

ABEL-

or,

CRACKED. —

# DREAMS

THERE can be comparatively little question that the place ordinarily occupied by dreams in literature is peculiarly unreal and unsatisfying. When the hero tells us that "last night he dreamed a dream," we are quite certain from the perfect and decorative character of the dream that he made it up at breakfast. The dream is so reasonable that it is quite impossible. An angel came to him and opened before him a scroll inscribed with some tremendous moral truth; a knight in armour rode past him declaring some ideal quest; the phantom of his mother arose to warn him from some imminent sin. Dreams like these are (with occasional exceptions) practically unknown in the lawless kingdoms of the night. A dream is scarcely ever rounded to express faultlessly some faultless idea. An angel might indeed open a scroll before the dreamer, but it would probably be inscribed with some remark about excursion trains to Brighton; a knight in armour might ride by him, but it would be impossible to deny that the most salient fact about that warrior was the fact that he was wearing three hats; his mother might indeed appear to the dreamer, and give him the tenderest and most elevated counsel, but it would be impossible for the loftiest ethical comfort to entirely obscure the fact that her nose was growing longer and longer every minute. Dreams have a kind of hellish ingenuity and energy in the pursuit of the inappropriate; the most omniscient and cunning artist never took so much trouble or achieved such success in finding exactly the word that was right or exactly the action that was significant, as this midnight lord of misrule can do in finding exactly the word that is wrong and exactly the action that is meaningless. The object of art is to subordinate the detail that is incidental to the tendency which is general. The object of a dream appears to be so to develop itself that some utterly futile and half-witted detail shall gradually devour all the other details of the vision. The flower upon the wall-paper just behind the head of Napoleon Buonaparte becomes brighter and brighter until we see nothing but a flower; the third waistcoat button of our best friend grows larger and larger until it is the great round sun of a revolving cosmos.

Thus at first sight it would seem that the lord of dreams was the eternal opponent of art. He seems to be to the æsthetic system what Satan is to the religious system, an unconquerable enemy, an irreducible minimum. The prigs of art who in this period erect their impeccable edifice, with even more than the gravity of the prigs of religion, have to deal with this mighty underworld of man in which their new rules are set as much at naught as the old ones, which is as careless of the modern canons of pleasure as of the ancient canons of pain. Asleep the artist is in the hands of an enchantress of ugliness who makes him love the discordant and hate the beautiful. In that realm the landscape painter paints monstrous landscapes, mingling scarlet and purple; in that realm the musician devises torturing melodies, and the architect top-heavy cathedrals.

So far as the forms and modes of art are concerned this is indeed true. The translucently allegorical dreams so often narrated in romance are essentially inconceivable. When the aged priest in a story narrates his dream, in which the imagery is dignified and the message plain, we are free to yield finally to a conviction that must have long been growing on us, and conclude that he is a somewhat distinguished liar. Dreams may have infinite meanings, but those meanings are not conveyed obviously by communicative mothers and candid angels. The Bible is an excellent place to look for a wisdom and morality older than mere words and ideals, and there is certainly far more truth in the old Biblical version of the nature of dreams which made them inscrutable and somewhat grotesque parables requiring particular persons to interpret them. If great spiritual truths are conveyed by dreams, they must certainly be conveyed as they were to Pharaoh or Nebuchadnezzar by farcical mysteries of clay-footed images and lean cows eating fat ones.

But there is another and far deeper manner in which dreams definitely correspond to art. Nothing is more remarkable in some of the great artistic masterpieces of the world than their startling deficiency in much of that sense of grace and proportion which goes nowadays by the name of art. If art were really what some contemporary critics represent it, a matter of the faultless arrangement of harmonies and transitions, Shakespeare would certainly not be anything like so great an artist as the last poetaster in Fleet Street who published a series of seven sonnets on seven varieties of grey sunset. Shakespeare often suffers from too much inventiveness; that which clogs us and trips us up in his masterpieces is not so much inferior work as irrelevant brilliancy; not so much failures as fragments of other masterpieces. Dickens was designless without knowing or caring; Sterne was designless by design. Yet these great works which mix up abstractions fit for an epic with fooleries not fit for a pantomime, which clash the sword with the red-hot poker, which present such a picture of literary chaos as might be produced if the characters in every book from *Paradise Lost* to *Pickwick* broke from their covers and mingled in one mad romance—these great works have assuredly a unity of their own or they would not be works of art. The unity which they have is a unity which when properly understood gives us the key of almost the whole of literary æsthetics: it is the same unity that we find in dreams. There is one unity which we do find in dreams. It binds together all their brutal inconsequence and all their moonstruck anti-climaxes. It makes the unimaginable nocturnal farce which begins with a saint choosing parasols and ends with a policeman shelling peas, as rounded and single a harmony as some poet's roundel upon a passion flower. This unity is the absolute unity of emotion. If we wish to experience pure and naked feeling we can never experience it so really as in that unreal land. There the passions seem to live an outlawed and abstract existence, unconnected with any facts or persons. In dreams we have revenge without any injury, remorse without any sin, memory without any recollections, hope without any prospect. Love, indeed, almost proves itself a divine thing by the logic of dreams; for in a dream every material circumstance may alter, spectacles may grow on a baby, and moustaches on a maiden aunt, and yet the great sway of one tyrannical tenderness may never cease. Our dream may begin with the end of the world, and end with a picnic at Hampton Court, but the same rich and nameless mood will be expressed by the falling stars and by the crumbling sandwiches. In a dream daisies may glare at us like the eyes of demons. In a dream lightning and conflagration may warm and soothe us like our own fireside. In this sub-conscious world, in short, existence betrays itself; it shows that it is full of spiritual forces which disguise themselves as lions and lamp-posts, which can as easily disguise themselves as butterflies and Babylonian temples. The essential unity of a dream, which is never broken or impaired, is the unity of its attitude towards God, wistful or vacant, or grateful, or rebellious or assured.

Surely this unity of dreams was the unity which underlay the old wild masterpieces of literature. The plays of Shakespeare, for example, may be full of incidental discords, but not one of them ever fails to convey its aboriginal sentiment, that life is as black as the tempest or as green as the greenwood. It is said that art should represent life. So indeed it should, but it labours under the primary disadvantage that no man has seen life at any time. Long records of Whitechapel crime, long rows of Brixton villas, the words which one clerk says to another clerk, the despatches that one diplomatist writes to another diplomatist, none of these things even approach to being life. For life the man of science, even if he lives in the very heart of Brixton, is still searching with a microscope. Life dwells alone in our very heart of hearts, life is one and virgin and unconjured, and sometimes in the watches of the night speaks in its own terrible harmony.

STILTON & MILTON

—or Literature in the 17th & 20th Centuries.

Pardon, dear Lady, if this Christmas time,
The convalescent Bard in halting rhyme
Thanks you for that great thought that still entwines
The Wicked Grocer with more wicked lines
These straggling Crayon lines — who cares for these
Who knows the difference between chalk and cheese?

Not wholly sound the saw, accounted sure,
That weak things perish and strong things endure:
Milton, six volumes on my groaning shelves,
May groan till Judgement Day and flhave themselves
As, harsh with leaden type and leathery pride,
Puritan Bards must groan at Christmas Tide:

My table groans with Stilton — for a while
Paradise found not Lost, in Milton's style
Green as his Eden; as his Michael strong:
But O, my friend, it will not groan there long.

# STILTON AND MILTON

## OR LITERATURE IN THE 17TH. AND 20TH. CENTURIES

Pardon, dear Lady, if this Christmas time,
The Convalescent Bard in halting rhyme
Thanks you for that great thought that still entwines
The Wicked Grocer with more wicked lines;
These straggling Crayon lines—who cares for these,
Who knows the difference between Chalk and Cheese?

Not wholly sound the saw, accounted sure,
That weak things perish and strong things endure:
Milton, six volumes on my groaning shelves,
May groan till Judgement Day and please themselves
As, harsh with leaden type and leathery pride,
Puritan Bards must groan at Christmas tide:

My table groans with Stilton—for a while:
Paradise Found not Lost, in Milton's style
Green as his Eden; as his Michael strong:
But O, my friend, it will not groan there long.

91

# IN THE EVENING

IT is the little brown hour of twilight.
I pause between two dark houses,
    For there is a song in my heart.
If I could sing at this moment what I wish to sing,
The nations would crown me,
    If I were dumb ever afterwards.
For I am sure it would be the greatest song in the world,
And the song every one has been trying to sing
        Just now !
    But it will not come out.


# TRIOLET

I WISH I were a jelly fish
That cannot fall downstairs:
Of all the things I wish to wish
I wish I were a jelly fish
That hasn't any cares,
And doesn't even have to wish
" I wish I were a jelly fish
That cannot fall downstairs."

# THE END OF THE ANECDOTE

"ONCE upon a time," said the Oldest Inhabitant, "there was a good and wise man named George Stephenson, who discovered a beautiful thing called the Locomotive Steam Engine for Railways. And when he was making arrangements for it, a miserable Rustic raised the objection that it would be very awkward if a Cow——"

"Pray do not trouble yourself further," said the Youngest Inhabitant. "I know that story. I have heard that story before. Your friend George said that it would be very awkward for the Cow. And, for some reason I do not understand, he is considered to have scored more completely because he pronounced it Coo. Possibly so as to rhyme with Moo. A sort of repartee to the Ruminant, I imagine."

"Pardon me," replied the Oldest Inhabitant mildly. "You are in error. You do not know the story. You only know the beginning of the story. After George Stephenson had delivered his light-hearted reply about it being very awkward for the cow, the train went forward, the cow was killed in due course; and it was very awkward for the Rustic, who subsisted largely by consuming and selling the milk of the quadruped. The Rustic, therefore, was not so light-hearted. His state of mind was described as the Depression of Agriculture. But everybody was so happy in travelling in trains and making it awkward for cows that these morbid broodings were generally ignored. Then quite suddenly there broke out various things called Wars and

Revolutions; which nobody was expecting, because they had only happened at regular intervals in the Past and nobody had yet had any experience of them in the Future. And all the people living in the large happy town, who believed that milk originally came from large cans, were distressed to find no more cans being delivered at Paddington Station; until somebody told them that milk does not come from cans but from cows; and they began almost to wish that they had not made it so awkward for cows. By the time that a certain percentage of their babies had died they began almost to wish that they had cows of their own, or at least cows within comparatively easy access and not cut off from them by Wars and Revolutions. However, as a number of Progressives and Optimists eagerly explained to them, it was then Too Late. So the babies died and the land became desolate, as you see. A few lunatics lingered for a little while, earnestly and mechanically going through the motions of milking the Steam-Engine, but with no really hopeful results. But some say that the Steam-Engine still wanders over the plain like a lost spirit, singing its lonely song."

" Is that," asked the Youngest Inhabitant, " what is called the Railway Whistle? "

" We generally call it," replied the other, " The Tune the Old Cow Died Of."

Despair of Herod
on finding Children
Convalescing from the
—Massacre.

# THE WILD GOOSE CHASE AT THE KINGDOM OF THE BIRDS

by

G. K. Chesterton, J.D.C.

Illustrated by the author.

To Lawrence Solomon, J.D.C. who, though a critic, is still enough
of a critic to be fond of Fairy Tales.  This nonsense is affectionately
dedicated by Another Baby.

" Not on the vulgar mass
Called ' work ' must sentence pass . . .

Thoughts hardly to be packed
Into a narrow act,
Fancies that broke through language and escaped:
All I could never be
All men ignored in me
This I was worth to God, whose wheel the pitcher shaped."
BROWNING: *Rabbi Ben Ezra.*

["J. D. C." was the Junior Debating Club at St. Paul's
School—*Ed.*]

# THE WILD GOOSE CHASE

ONCE upon a time there lived in a certain village a little boy who was so dreamy and gentle by nature that it was the general opinion of the villagers that he couldn't, as they figuratively expressed it, "say boh to a goose." Why this ceremony should be selected as a test of the average minimum of personal courage, he never could make out, and nor can I. But, being resolved to show that he was not unfit for this perilous venture, he went one evening to the village green at sunset, where a number of geese were congregated, to pronounce the mysterious monosyllable.

"Boh," observed the Little Boy, addressing the first biped, with all the earnestness of scientific enquiry. The goose received it in dignified silence, and the Little Boy went on to the next and said, "Boh," but no effects followed. When, however, he came to the third, who was a wilder and shyer bird than the others, and tried the experiment on him, he fluttered, flapped his wings and flew away in a straight line towards the setting sun. The white geese looked superciliously after it and then at each other and waddled back over the village green, observing that it was only a wild goose and perhaps one could expect no better. But the Little Boy was already far away.

What impulse led him to chase the wild goose he never knew, but with the persistence of scientific enquiry he scampered through the streets in pursuit of the bird that fluttered on before him. Nothing could stop his course. He cleared the stile, he climbed over the palings, he upset three vestrymen and a beadle (though that, of course, was quite right), he ran out of the town gates and out into the fields and lanes, lonely in the evening. As he paused for a moment to take breath under an elm-tree, he saw a titmouse just fluttering into its nest among its fat little family. "It is evening," observed the titmouse, "and I and my family go to rest. It is very comfortable here. Where are you going, little boy?" And the Little Boy sighed as he answered, "Yes, a home is very comfortable, but now I have no home. I am seeking the wild goose that has flown westward towards the sunset." And after bowing to the maternal titmouse and patting the little ones on the head, he ran westward once more. And now as the sun went down through rose-red fire to bury itself in violet mist, he reached a wonderful place where the gorgeous light of sunset glittered on the plumage of gorgeous birds, moving proudly about spaces of green park. Here peacocks spread their green-eyed fantails before him, golden pheasants bowed their necks under his hand and the air above him glittered with the emerald and ruby-throated humming-birds, whirring round in ceaseless movement. Pausing under a magnificent flowering fruit-tree, he asked a Bird of Paradise if she had seen a wild goose pass there lately. The " Paradisia Apoda " rustled through all its flaming feathery appanage and observed gravely and severely. " If you are seeking a wild goose, sir, I can assure you that he has not been here. We do not visit them." And the royal lady closed her eyes and looked as if she only wanted a pair of eye-glasses to make her complete.

A pea-hen swept up to her and said smiling, " Oh, pray excuse me, but the band is going to commence; and I know you dote on music." " Oh yes," said the Bird of Paradise, closing her eyes again. " Frivolous creature," she muttered as the pea-hen swept away. " Supercilious old owl," snapped the pea-hen under her breath. Meanwhile the Little Boy had moved forward, anxious to know what was meant by " the band." He found it impersonated by one shabby little brown nightingale, who every evening gave a musical performance to the rapture of the assembled company.

After the performance the Little Boy got a word with the poor little nightingale.

"Whence have you come?" said the poor musician. "Have you come from the calm woods and the fields and the sweet country lanes? I can remember when I too was free in the free forests and sang my songs as the free gift of God. But now I have these grand patrons and the beauty of the woods has died out of me till you for a moment brought it back. In God's name do not linger here. Flee westward to seek your wild goose and do not lose your work as I have done." And so sorrowful was the look in the eyes of the little old songster that the Little Boy broke into tears as he said farewell and ran from the place. All he could gather about the object of his search was that he had better go and ask the Owl that dwelt in the Forest of Dead Leaves in a deep twilight of meditation. An hour after he had emerged from the Park he came to the Forest of Dead Leaves, a weird brown twilight of thick trees, amid which the ground was heaped and littered with drifts of dry leaves, through which he waded and struggled waistdeep for hours before he came to the great mystic oak in the dark shadow of whose branches he could dimly see the solemn round eyes of the gigantic owl. When she saw the Little Boy, she blinked several times and enquired in a muffled voice what he wanted. "I came to you for some information," replied the Little Boy "as I heard you were very wise."

"Too whoo! and you heard right. Do you see these brown leaves heaped thick throughout the forest? They are the leaves that have fallen from this Tree of Knowledge, and I am waiting till they are withered and worth touching. Too whoo; they may think themselves very fine with their bright crests and plumage, but they will never know what I do. What do you want to know?"

"I am seeking the wild goose," replied the Little Boy, "that fled westward towards the sunset."

The Owl blinked, coughed a little and said, "The wild goose, or Anserferus, as it is scientifically termed, is an inhabitant of many parts of the globe. It was of the plumes of this animal that the archers of the Middle Ages . . ."

"Yes, yes," said the Little Boy, impatiently, "but I want to know where it can be found. It fled westward half an hour before sunset."

"Sunset," replied the Owl, smoothing down her feathers, "is caused by the orb of the earth moving in its revolution. . . ."

"Confound its revolution," said the naughty Little Boy. "Cannot you tell me where the thing I want is?"

"Well, what *do* you want?" asked the Owl with a stare.

And all the Little Boy could answer was, "I want the beautiful wild goose that flew towards the sunset."

"And what do you want with a wild goose?"

"Well, I want it," began the Little Boy, "because—because it was so wild and natural."

"Was not the titmouse you left behind natural?"

"Yes," said the Little Boy, puzzled. "But I followed it because it was beautiful."

"Were not the Bird of Paradise and the Peacock as beautiful?" asked the Owl.

"I think," said the Little Boy at last in a brown study, "I seem to have followed because I couldn't get it."

"Logical," sniffed the Owl.

"No," replied the Boy, "not logical, only natural. I looked at the white bird flapping far away against the fiery sunset and I seemed to long to spend my whole life in seeking for it in the strange sunset lands. I longed to follow it and find where it lived and all about it simply because it seemed as if the chase might last for ever."

The Little Boy paused for a reply, stared, shook the tree and woke up the owl from a sound nap which she had indulged in during the mystical explanation above. "What do you want?" asked the owl sleepily. "Don't disturb me. I'm thinking. Don't you know I'm the wisest person in the world?"

"You are the most useless rubbish in the world," said the rude Little Boy. "I come to you for simple directions and you give me extracts from dictionaries. I come to you in search of my vanished ideal and you tell me I am not logical. I tell you the feelings of my nature and you go to sleep while I am speaking. Oh, it were better to be the little titmouse that hops and twitters its happy little life and dies than this miserable old spirit of darkness." And with that he turned and strode away, leaving behind him the Owl of Learning and the Forest of Dead Leaves. Just, however, as the indignant hootings of the old owl had died away in the distance he heard another loud "too whoo!" close to his ear. "What," he cried, "is there another owl here?"

"No," said a shrill voice from the same direction, with a caricature of his childish accent. "No. No owls here. Except you."

Looking round at the tree behind him, he beheld a thin black bird with a kind of furtive grin and a cruel look in his eyes.

"Who—who are you?" asked the Little Boy falteringly.

"I—, I am—a—the Mocking Bird," replied the bird, imitating him once more. "You have been talking to that unconscionable old imbecile, the owl. Too whoo! Too whoo! I'm the wisest person in the world. What did you want with her?"

"I am looking for a wild goose," replied the Little Boy, beginning to be a trifle tired of the answer, "that has fled towards the sunset."

"Cackle, cackle," said the Mocking Bird. "Birds of a feather flock together. I don't wonder you want to flock with a goose."

The Little Boy flushed scarlet. "I don't know why you should speak to me——"

"Go it," grinned the Mocking Bird. "Do the virtuous indignant business. It pays nowadays. About the only thing to be said for it. Go it. Charge, Chester, charge, etc. Ha, ha."

"Who are you to speak to me in this way?" asked the Boy fiercely.

"I'm a cynic," chuckled the Mocking Bird, "and cynics are allowed to say anything. I suppose it is a kind of recognition that they are the only people who speak the truth. I'll prove we speak the truth. You're a fool."

"Hold your tongue!" shouted the Little Boy, clenching his fists.

"Can't be done. Heroic style won't do for you," said the Mocking Bird placidly. "Your voice, my dear boy, is too juvenile."

"My voice may be juvenile," retorted the Little Boy, "but it is my own. I have something of my own to say and my natural voice to say it in. I am not like the miserable misanthrope who can do nothing but pick holes in his own versions of other people's voices. I would as soon be the echo on a blank garden wall."

Not having anything particular to answer to this and being irritated and a trifle confused, the Mocking Bird only said excitedly, "Too whoo, cockadoodledoomeowcackle-bowwow, confound it," and ran into a hole in the tree, while the Little Boy continued his onward march. He had emerged from the outskirts of the wood and come out on a broad, bleak upland, beyond which the sunset was fading in level clouds. He had not walked far when he heard a scream and there sidled up to him, in a semi-tipsy manner, a disreputable-looking large bird with a crooked beak, a long bare neck with a ruff of dirty white feathers, a smart red crest and a leering eye.

" How de do," he observed hoarsely.

" How do you do," said the Little Boy meekly, but not much liking his company.

" Coming my way ? " asked the Vulture, taking out a cigar. " See *our* tree. Better job than those," and he jerked his thumb-claw in the direction of the forest. " Come with me. Introduce you to the fellers——There they are ! " And he nodded in the direction of the sunset against which there now rose dark and grim the outline of a gibbet, almost obscured by the crowds of vultures that flocked round it. " Here we are," said the Vulture. " Lots of fellers. Writing fellers. Doosid original fellers. I'm a doosid original feller."

The Little Boy thought he was.

"Yes," said the vulture. "This is where I hang out," though the last expression would have more properly applied to another part of his establishment. "Won't you come in?"

"N-no thank you," said the Little Boy hurriedly. "I think

this is my way," which was not strictly true, as he ran three miles and a half out of his way in order to give a wide berth to the Tree of the Vultures.

And as the moon came slowly up over the moor he wandered among the ruins of an old building in which no living thing stirred, save flocks of lugubrious looking ravens that darkly flapped and croaked round the turrets. After wandering about for some time he fell into conversation with a large, gaunt, disappointed-looking bird, of whom he asked his question in the formula of which the reader has probably got as tired as he had.

"Wild goose?" replied the Raven wearily. "I don't know. There's nothing worth going after nowadays. Look at this abbey. Its all tumbling down. What can the world be coming to? Take my advice, little boy, leave things alone. There's nothing worth touching in these days. Croak, croak."

And shaking his large head mournfully, he blinked and went to sleep. "Croak, croak," cried all the ravens fretfully as the Little Boy passed slowly out of the ruins and struck westwards once more.

For years and years he wandered over the earth, past rivers and cities and mountain-ranges, until one day he found himself on the wild slopes of a mountain, above which incline a line of dark cliffs jutted, overshadowing the base of the hill.

After wandering about disconsolately for some time he was attracted by the low moaning and sobbing of a living thing. Stooping down he found it was a starling, fluttering close to the ground.

"What is the matter, poor little bird?" he asked, and forgot even to ask after the wild goose; and the starling told him that his brother had just been carried off by a ferocious eagle, who had swooped down from his nest upon the cliff's edge. "There he is," cried the starling, and looking up he saw a large bird flapping on the cliff with a smaller one struggling in his grasp. The Little Boy, not being acquainted with the law of the success of the fittest in Nature, rushed forward, wildly clambered up the cliff and continued at the imminent risk of his neck to get onto the ledge with the oppressor and his victim. Seizing the eagle by the throat and claw, he forced it back against the rock, while the starling flew away joyfully to join his companion, and the eagle flapped sulkily back to his nest. Just then, as the Little Boy hung clinging to the edge of the cliff and wondering how he should get down again, he saw with a start that almost loosed his hold, gleaming for a moment amid the rock-rooted brake and thicket above his head, the white wings of the wild goose. In a moment he was on the ground above, just in time to see the wild goose disappear over the next swell of ground. When he had passed this, he saw spread before him a mighty valley, watered by broad rivers and clothed with deep forests, and beyond it a range of mountains in the distance, culminating in one central, snow-crested peak, upon which he could see perched the white shining bird that he sought. And after it he set forth across the mighty valley.

Years passed and he had grown to a strong man, who might have won the hands of ladies or tilted in the tournaments of Kings, but that he was still upon the quest of his life, when he arrived at the mountain of the wild goose. Bare-headed, with a staff in his hand, with a wild hope in his eyes, he climbed the rocky slopes, until late upon a summer evening he clambered close beneath the topmost crag whereon sat the wild goose. And even as he stretched out his hand to touch it, it started and flew far from him, vanishing over the twilight sea, and he stood on the lonely crest, with a sheer precipice beneath him. And he gave a great groan and sank with his face buried in his hands.

"It is gone," he murmured. "Gone for ever. And my youth is gone, which I wasted, and my strength which I exhausted for it. The graves are green on all the friends I loved. I am alone

in a strange land, where all are strangers.  My hope is gone, for which I gave up everything.  Heaven has had no pity on me."  And then all was silence.

"Yes," said a strange voice above him.  "Heaven has pitied you, and for your sake time itself shall be defied.  I am the Spirit of the Past.  I am come to give you back everything and to wipe out all your sorrows.  I am come to tear the page of all your toils and wanderings out of the very book of what has been, and make you once more a little boy playing upon a village green and not thinking of a wild goose."

The wanderer lifted his head and gazed dreamily over the sea and a strange light grew in his eyes.

"No, spirit, no," he said quickly.  "It is better as it is.  I will not have it so."

And with that the dim spirit of the Past moved slowly towards the far-off hills of his home.

But over the darkening sea there came a sudden, strange, wordless song as of a flight of wild birds, and a glimmer of white wings seemed floating towards him.  He gave a great cry and leapt forward; and no man ever saw him again on earth.

And I have not said whether he ever found the wild goose, and the story ends abruptly.  And must not all stories of brave lives and long endeavours and weary watching for the ideal so end, until all be ended?

I cannot tell you whether he found what he sought.  I have told you that he sought it.

# THE ARTISTIC SIDE

In the days of my early youth, in the days of the Yellow Book and the Green Carnation, there were many idle fancies that were quite harmless because they were fanciful, as well as one or two which hardened into evil imaginations. A curious legend has arisen that the Yellow Book, with its grave contributions by Henry James or its innocent contributions by Kenneth Graham, was a book of black, or at least of yellow magic. As a matter of fact, the Yellow Book might almost have been a Blue Book, so far as the harmless and humdrum sobriety of much of its printed matter went; and even the Green Carnation was not so green as it was painted. These things were seen afterwards in the lurid light that shone backwards from the shameful illumination of one individual career; but at the time most of us saw very little harm in them; or at least very little harm of this particular kind. The peacock's feather of the aesthete had not yet proved itself a true type of ill-luck; and a man might be irritated with Whistler for posing so persistently as a Butterfly, without associating him with the real moth that corrupts; or any of the subsequent corruption.

Among the pleasing fancies that occurred to us in those early days was a sense of the poetry of London; and, in the days when I wrote a fortunately forgotten work called " The Napoleon of Notting Hill," I quite honestly felt that I was adorning a neglected thing, when I felt impelled to write about lamp-posts as one-eyed giants or hansom cabs as yawning dragons with two flaming optics, or painted omnibuses as coloured ships or castles, or all the rest of it. And, now, after many years of controversy and complications, and collisions with all sorts of other questions, I come back to the same feeling in a new way, but with something of an undiminished freshness. I still hold, every bit as firmly as when I wrote " The Napoleon of Notting Hill," that the suburbs ought to be either glorified by romance and religion or else destroyed by fire from heaven, or even by firebrands from the earth. I still hold that it is the main earthly business of a human being to make his home, and the immediate surroundings of his home, as symbolic and significant to his own imagination as he can; whether the home be in Notting Hill or Nicaragua, in Palestine or in Pittsburgh. But an experience of the mingled strands of modern life has led me to consider the problem in a slightly different way; though I will claim to have added to my views rather than abandoned them.

I know no better exercise in that art of wonder, which is the life of man and the beginning of the praise of God, than to travel in a train through a long dark almost uninterrupted tunnel: until the traveller has grown almost accustomed to dusk and a dead blank background of brick. At last, after long stretches and at long intervals, the wall will suddenly break in two, and give a glowing glimpse of the land of the living. It may be a chasm of daylight showing a bright and busy street. It may be a similar flash of light on a long lonely road of poplars, with a solitary human figure plodding across the vast countryside. I know not which of the two gives a more startling stab of human vitality. Sometimes the grey façade is broken by the lighted windows of a house, almost overhanging the railway-line; and for an instant we look deep into a domestic interior; chamber within chamber of a glowing and coloured human home. That is the way in which objects ought to be seen; separate; illuminated; and above all, contrasted against blank night or bare walls; as indeed these living creations do stand eternally contrasted with the colourless chaos out of which they came. Travelling in this fashion, the other day, I was continually haunted, and almost tormented, with an impression that I could not disentangle; nor am I at all confident that I can disentangle it here.

It seemed to me that I saw very strange sights; which ought to have been significant sights. I looked suddenly through an open window into a little room that was filled with blue light; something much bluer than we see in moonlight, even once in a blue moon. It came apparently from the blue shade that completely hooded a lamp standing on the table; there was nothing else on the table but an open book, which gleamed almost pale blue in that bleak luminosity. There was nobody there; there was nothing else. And I had an indescribable subconscious sense that it ought to mean something; and there massed vaguely at the back of my mind, like blue clouds, the colours that cling about the Blessed Virgin in the old pictures and the visions seen in narrow rooms and cells. Then again I saw a square patch of burning red, which was but the red curtain covering a lighted room. But there was a shadow that moved sharply across it, lifting long arms, arms of an unnatural exaggerated length, and making the black pattern of a cross upon the burning scarlet. It was impossible not to feel that somebody had made a signal to the train. And yet somebody had only stretched his arms, probably with a yawn, before going indifferently to bed. All along that night journey there were these signals signifying nothing. And I grew conscious, in a way quite beyond expression, that there is indeed a poetry of modern life, and of the modern cities; but it is in some strange way a poetry of misfits; a tangle of misunderstood messages; an alphabet all higgledy-piggledy in a heap. Beautiful things ought to mean beautiful things. And the case for simpler conditions is that, on the whole, they do. That indestructibility of religion, and even of ritualism, which puzzles the poor old rationalist so much, is not a little due to the fact that in ritual, for the first time, modern men see forms and colours placed where they mean something. Anybody can see why the priest's vestment on common days is green like the common fields, and on martyrs' days red as blood. But that blood-red curtain I saw from the train either commemorated no martyrdom; or the man crucified within did not know that his martyrdom was commemorated.

WAT TILER

OR, A TILE LOOSE.

AS I WOULD LIKE TO BE

AS I AM

# A BALLADE OF THE GROTESQUE

I was always the elephant's friend,
   I never have caused him to grieve;
Though monstrous and mighty to rend
   He was fed from the fingers of Eve,
   He is wise, but he will not deceive,
He is kind in his wildest career;
   But still I will say, with his leave,
The shape is decidedly queer.

I was light as a penny to spend,
   I was thin as an arrow to cleave,
I could stand on a fishing-rod's end
   With composure, though on the *qui vive;*
   But from Time, all a-flying to thieve
The suns and the moons of the year,
   A different shape I receive;
The shape is decidedly queer.

I am proud of the world as I wend,
   What hills could omnipotence heave,
I consider the heaven's blue bend
   A remarkable feat to achieve;
   —But think of the Cosmos—conceive
The universe—system and sphere,
   I must say with my heart on my sleeve,
The shape is decidedly queer.

# BALLADE OF THE GROTESQUE

Prince, Prince, what is this I perceive
On the top of your collar appear?
You say it's your face, you believe,
. . . The shape is decidedly queer.

# A SONG OF WILD FRUIT

*To D. E. C. with thanks*

THE Pineapple knows nothing
Of the Apple or the Pine,
The Grape-Fruit is a fruit: but not
The God's fruit of the Vine;
And Grape-nuts are not even Nuts
For the Hygienic Hut
Where the nut-crank with the nut-crackers
Is cracking his own nut.

Far in the land of Nonsense Names
These antic fruits were born,
Where men gather grapes of thistles
And the figs grow on the thorn.
And Ananias named the fruit
That Frenchmen call Ananas;
And all the Plantains are a plant,
And . . . No! We have Bananas!

# PAINTS IN A PAINT-BOX

THERE has often arisen before my mind the image of an individual who should collect with laborious care articles which no other person valued and make an exhaustive classification of things which everyone else regarded as insignificant and inane. This being might have a magnificent and futile pre-eminence in many enterprises. He might have the finest collection of disused cigar ends in the world. He might accumulate pipe ashes and the parings of lead pencils with an enthusiasm and a poetry worthy of a better cause. He might, if he were a millionaire, carry this immense crusade into even larger matters. He might build great museums in which nothing was exhibited except lost umbrellas and bad pennies. He might found important papers and magazines in which nothing was recorded except unimportant things; in which stunning head lines announced the loss of three burnt matches out of an ash tray and long and philosophical leading articles were devoted to such questions as the Christian names of the Fulham omnibus conductors, or the number of green window-blinds in the Harrow Road. If a man did seriously devote himself to these inanities he would unquestionably be the object of a great deal of derision. Nevertheless, if he chose to turn round upon us and defend his position, we should suddenly realise that our whole civilisation was as moonstruck as his hobby. He would say with truth that there was, philosophically speaking, as much to be said for collecting the ferrules of gentlemen's umbrellas as for collecting books or banknotes. For all essential purposes there is no reason which can be offered for the preference which man-kind exhibits for one material rather than another. It is impossible to suggest a single valid reason why gold should be more expensive than a genuinely rich red mud. It is impossible to say why a precious stone should be more valued than a copying-ink pencil or an old green bottle, which are both more useful and more picturesque. Almost all the theories which profess to explain this paradox from the metaphysical point of view have failed entirely. It is commonly said, for example, that materials are valued on account of their rarity. Clearly, however, this cannot be main-tained. There are a great many things more rare than gold and silver; however small may be the chances for anyone of us of picking up half-a-sovereign in the gutter, the chances that we should pick up a latch-key tied up with red ribbon, or a copy of *The Times* descriptive of the introduction of the first Home Rule Bill, are even less. Yet people do not make a private museum of latch-keys with red ribbons or boast of a unique collection of copies of *The Times* for that particular date of 1885. Those who speak of rarity as the essence of value seem scarcely to realise how prodigious are the consequences of their view. The things in this world which are thoroughly insignificant are precisely the things which are singularly rare. It is very rare for a solicitor with a red moustache born in Devonshire to lend 1s. 6d. to the nephew of a Scotch cloth-merchant residing in Clement's Inn; such a thing perhaps has only happened once, if at all; yet we do not write the incident in letters of gold, or attach any particular importance to any incidentals, rags or relics, which may have been found to be commemorative of the spot where it occurred. Mere rarity certainly is not the test of value. If it were so, gold would be less valuable than many varieties of street mud, and beautiful things upon the whole much less valuable than ugly ones. The fact of the matter is, that mankind has selected certain unmeaning objects as things of value without either intrinsic or comparative criticism. It has made one material infinitely more valuable than another material by a mere process of selecting one kind of mud from another. In many respects the current conception of the substance which is valuable is decidedly an inferior one. Value, for example, almost entirely centres around metals, which are the dullest and most uncommunicative, the most material, of all earthly things. They belong to the mineral creation, which is the very canaille of the cosmic order. It is extraordinary when one comes to think of it that so thoroughly base a thing as gold metal should be the form in which all our most human and humanising tendencies are bound up. Whenever we apply for payment in cash, we fulfil almost to the point of detail the word of the parable, we ask for bread and we receive a stone.

Again, the theory that materials are valued on account of their beauty will not support criticism. There are a great many objects which are more beautiful than precious objects. Peacocks' feathers are more beautiful, and autumn leaves and split firewood and clean copper. Nevertheless, it has not occurred to any person to swagger in a purse-proud manner over his possession of firewood or to cling to every advantage which could be founded upon copper. The miser who should spend a laborious life in hoarding and counting the autumn leaves has, I think, yet to be born.

Substances have, however, a real intrinsic spirituality. Materials are not likely to be despised except by materialists. Children, for example, are fully conscious of a certain mystical, and yet practical, quality in the things they handle; they love the essential quality of an object chivalrously, and for its own sake. A child has an ingrained fancy for coal, not for the gross materialistic reason that it builds up fires by which we cook and are warmed, but for the infinitely nobler and more abstract reason that it blacks his fingers. In almost all the old primitive literatures we find the presence of this splendid love of materials for their own sake. We find no delicate and cunning combinations of colour, such as those which are the essence of our latter-day art, but we find a gigantic appetite for materials linked with their own natural characteristics, for red gold, and green grass; not the taste for green gold and red grass which marks so much contemporary literature. They did not require either contrast or harmony to tickle their æsthetic hunger. They loved the redness of wine or the white splendour of the sword in all their virginity and loveliness, a single splash of crimson or silver upon the black background of old Night.

The poetry of substances exists, and it takes no account of the ordinary codes of value. Gold is certainly a less fascinating substance than silver. And even silver is to the spirit which retains its childhood less fascinating than lead. Lead is a truly epic substance; it contains every quality that could be required for that purpose. In colour it is the most delicate tint of dimmed silver, a kind of metallic splendour under a perpetual cloud; in consistency again it unites two of the antagonistic and indispensable elements of a fascinating substance. It is at once robust and malleable, it bends and it resists; we have the same feeling towards a stiff layer of lead that we have towards destiny. It is stiff, yet it yields sufficiently to make us fancy that it might yield altogether. Another substance which presents in a somewhat different way the same contradiction is common wood. It is the most fascinating and the most symbolic of substances, since it has just enough essential toughness to resist the amateur, and just enough pliability to become like a musical instrument in the hands of the expert. Working in wood is the supreme example of creation; creation in a material which resists just enough and not an iota too much. It was surely no wonder that the greatest who ever wore the form of man was a carpenter.

There remains one definite order of materials which have to the imaginative eye far more essential value than any jewels. All pigments and colour materials have one supreme advantage over mere diamonds and amethysts. They are, so to speak, ancestors as well as descendants; they propagate an infinite progeny of images and ideas. If we look at a solid bar of blue chalk we do not see a thing merely mechanical and final. We see bound up in that blue column a whole fairyland of potential pictures and tales. No other material object gives us this sense of multiplying itself. If we leave a cigar in a corner we do not expect that we shall find it next day surrounded by a family of cigarettes. A diamond ring does not contribute in any way to the production of innumerable necklaces and bracelets. But the chalks in a box, or the paints in a paint-box, do actually embrace in themselves an infinity of new possibilities. A cake of prussian blue contains all the sea stories in the world, a cake of emerald green encloses a hundred meadows, a cake of crimson is compounded of forgotten sunsets. Some day, for all we know, this eternal metaphysical value in chalks and paints may be recognised as of monetary value; men will proudly show a cake of chrome yellow in their rings, and a cake of ultramarine in their scarfpins. There is no saying what wild fashions the changes of time may make; a century may find us economising in pebbles and collecting straws. But whatever may come, the essential ground of this habit will remain the same as the essential ground of all the religions, that we can only take a sample of the universe, and that that sample, even if it be a handful of dust (which is also a beautiful substance), will always assert the magic of itself, and hint at the magic of all things.

*Poker Patience An Impression.*

# A FRAGMENT

I EARNESTLY hope that all children will spoil this book by painting the illustrations. I wanted to do this myself but the publishers[1] would not let me. But let the colours you lay on be violent, gorgeous, terrific colours, because my feelings are like that.

I have chosen the wonderful story of my friend the Admiral and his companions to tell you, because of all the wise and good men I have known and loved the Admiral was, I do not hesitate to say, the easiest to paint with water-colours. You have only to colour his cocked hat and laced coat a strong prussian blue, and his trousers the same, leaving room for a great many gold buttons and gold stripes, but be careful or it will all go green and trickling. His face, which is rather like an eagle's or a lean parrot's, may be as burning red as you like, his hair and eyebrows white, and under them a pair of eyes, for which you must consult the little slip of directions they sell you with the paint box, to find out what colours are commonly used to express a look of ancient suffering transfigured with immortal hope. You will find the slip under the paint brushes. The Admiral, you see, was a martyr of science, a pilgrim of truth, one of those who live and die for one moment that may never come, the sight of a cape or the sudden colouring of a precipitate: if you do not understand the language, I can only roughly render it by the phrase that there is no fool like an old fool. Shall I tell you the search

[1] Who were these criminal publishers? Not we. We publish this unfinished fragment exactly as it was found tossed away amidst a vast heap of his papers [S. & W.].

128

of the Admiral's life? He wished to discover America. His gay and thoughtless friends, who could not understand him, pointed out that America had already been discovered, I think they said by Christopher Columbus, some time ago, and that there were big cities of Anglo-Saxon people there already, New York and Boston and so on. But the Admiral explained to them, kindly enough, that this was nothing to do with it. They might have discovered America, but he had not: he would take nothing superstitiously or on authority but wished to verify everything for himself. He had no proof even that " this island " as he used to call it, existed. But if it did, as many earnest men declared, " what dull stay-at-home credulity " he said " will compare with my victorious ecstasy, when I first see its purple peaks rise benignant in the sunset seas? "

But the tragedy of the Admiral was that he could never hit America. After vast calculations conducted in a lonely tower by the seashore, he would again and again start due west from Ireland in a straight line feeling sure that now he must hit North or South America somewhere. But he always found himself somewhere round by India or up against the coast of Norway, and recognized with a slight feeling of annoyance that some minute detail in his calculations had been wrong. On his last voyage he had seemed on the brink of success and had stood in the prow reciting a grand poem of his own composition to a dim blue promontory in which he recognised one of the capes of Greenland. But it is idle to deny that the general feeling was damped somehow, when they discovered it was the Cape of Good Hope. In short, the Admiral was one of those who keep the world young.

The Admiral's great friend was the Professor. He also is easy to paint, but it is cheaper to use ink for his black coat and hat. His face, which was long and lantern-jawed, was vivid yellow, just like a new artistic magazine (though he was not vain about it) and he wore a pair of enormous green spectacles that made him look like some unpleasant insect. He also carried a blue umbrella. He said that his dominating trait was a love of animals. He liked to have them round him, and sometimes stuck pins in them to make them stay. People told queer stories like fairy tales about the way he could charm fish up on shore with a song, like the Pied Piper. It is certain that he was often found sitting on the shore when the day broke, with heaps of dead fish all round him, each fish still wearing an expression of artistic rapture. But they were all dead. " I cannot," said the Professor, " live without those I love around me." The Professor did not want to go to America. That is why he sailed with the Admiral on the yacht. He wanted to go to one of the Cannibal Islands where there was a sort of slug. That slug gilded his day dreams, as the island America did those of the good Admiral.

Besides the Admiral, of course, there was the Crew.

The Crew was a small London gutter-boy, whom you may paint all the colours you like, especially black and blue. Yet, though his childhood had been hard and hungry, the Crew was the most cheerful person on board and sang the great compositions of the English music halls in many a wild and ignorant land that had not till then beheld the light of them. His clothing was unofficial, consisting chiefly of a pair of very loose trousers, tribal in their origin. He had run away to sea, partly to kill pirates and partly to visit the only brother who had ever been kind to him, who was in Australia, doing time. Like the Professor, therefore, he had quite a separate idea of where he was starting for. But they all three felt it was economical to go on one boat.

# A FRAGMENT

There was no other sign of life on the yacht, except indeed the owner of the yacht, a Duke I believe. He was a horsy young man with a large red and yellow chessboard coat and a horseshoe pin. He was quite harmless and had been ordered by his doctor to sail at once to the island of Madeira.

The night that they started on the remarkable voyage which is the subject of my story, the Admiral gave his customary dinner to the party at the Holborn Restaurant. The Crew was admitted, for the Admiral was a gentleman and consequently never thought of the fact. And I am not quite sure myself whether any of the wild adventures that followed was more thoroughly supernatural to the gutter-boy than that dinner, with its green and brown soups, its red and orange wines, its crystal ices and its fiery coffee. His face when partaking of all these was worth a hundred farces. It is an aged face ordinarily, its look of elfish wisdom and experience looking quite startling on the little swaggering body, and contrasting with the look of slightly lunatic simplicity on the faces of the Admiral and the Professor. But his face when hewing his way through the dinner had a look of tight, savage, conscientiously controlled hysteria, like a cavalry subaltern leading a charge.

When the last cigar was smoked out they bundled with all their luggage into a cab, and shot away through the million colours of a London night-scene. It was the hour when London becomes a city of the goblins, every lamp-post a one-eyed giant, every hansom-cab a yawning monster with two fiery eyes. In this hour and mood my story begins.

There was one peculiarity about the journey. Whenever and wherever they changed their position from cab to train or train to boat, the Admiral made a hurried calculation of the luggage and always got it wrong by one box over. Besides the Admiral's sword and telescope which he wore along with his uniform, the Professor's gun which he carried under his arm (lest he should be suddenly smitten with unrequited attachment to a partridge) and the red bundle of the Crew's belongings which he carried on the end of a stick, besides these, I say, the luggage should only consist of two boxes, a Gladstone bag belonging to the Duke and a medicine chest belonging to the Professor. But whenever the Admiral put the boxes in a row, and counted them carefully he found that there were three, not two. He was not sure: and counted them again from the other end, and again the number three resulted. The Admiral was just about to make an attempt to work it out by algebra and see whether there was really one box over, when the Duke always bundled him bodily into the train or boat, and the Admiral was forced to admit that it was no time for such abstruse problems. Five times at five successive stations did the poor Admiral put the boxes in a row in front of him and try to come to a serious and unbiased opinion about their number. But every time, as I say, the Duke dragged him off, boxes and all: so that it was not until they were actually on the yacht and the anchor weighed, that the Admiral had an opportunity of finally coming to the conclusion, not lightly or without deep feeling, that there were three boxes and therefore one box over.

It was a black box with silver corners, with no strap round it, but a strong lock. The question was, what was inside it?

It became quite an amusement for them in the beautiful summer evenings on deck, when the sky was a wall of gold and the sea a pavement of sapphire, to sit round the box in a circle and offer a number of theories about what might be inside it. The Admiral had seen a lot of life, the Professor was a scientific man, and the Duke had a vast acquaintance with detective stories—so between them a number of the most interesting possibilities were suggested. And really, when one comes to think of it, there are a large number of things which might be inside a big black box which you have never seen or heard of before. The Duke had a splendidly convincing history of it, something about an Italian ice-cream man and a murder on the Yorkshire Moors, but I have forgotten it, I am sorry to say, for really it might have been true. But for all that, the members of the party seemed much more convinced of the falsehood of each other's theories than of the finality of their own: and when in the night a loud scream was heard through the darkness, everyone knew that the Professor or the Admiral, lying sleepless in their bunks, had just thought of something else that might be in the black box.

But one night it was observed that the Crew was timidly drawing near the circle. He asked permission to speak, which was graciously extended. Then he said, not without emotion, that an idea had occurred to him which might result in the discovery of a means to obtain the secret. He had, he explained, heard a similar story. An uncle of his (one of those heroes of humble life who gain too little recognition) had been faced with a similar difficulty, that of desiring to know the contents of a box that had been sent him by post. He had eluded it by opening the box.

There was no cataclysm in Nature. The sea still shone like a sapphire floor, the skies like a golden wall. But the Admiral rose to his feet slowly and approached the boy.

"Take off my hat," said the Admiral imperatively, "take off my hat."

The Crew retreated in some bewilderment and alarm.

"Put on my boots," cried the Admiral wildly, "assume my

133

waistcoat. Accept my braces. Command my ship. Save us!"
And the Admiral fell on his knees before the Crew.

"Oh, Sir," said the boy, vaguely reminiscent of the Penny
Dreadfuls. "Sir, do not kneel to me. Get up yer blooming old
josser—get up."

"Adopt my socks," murmured the Admiral faintly, "adopt
my socks."

The Crew was almost in tears. "I can't command no ship,"
he said brokenly, "I ain't silly enough. Lor' bless yer, I knew
more badness when I was five years old than you'll know all your
born days, you blooming old cherub with a telescope. No, Cap'n,
I ain't good enough, people wouldn't do things for me like they
do 'em for you—lor' bless yer, they'd chuck me into the sea,
if I made such a fool of myself as you do. There—don't that
satisfy you?" And he turned tearfully toward the gangway.

The Duke was a man of few words. He listened to the
eulogium on the Admiral with a face of stone, but just as the boy
was descending the gangway a small and hard object hit him
on the head, sped on its errand by the powerful fingers of that
taciturn aristocrat.

It was half a sovereign.

The boy picked it up and hurled a last missile. "Garn—
yer've forgotten about openin' the box already."

The Admiral started. "This yacht must be saved from perils,"
he said solemnly. "It contains a Mind."

"Don't make him bumptious," growled the Duke. "He's
all right, but he ought to respect you."

"He has lived but fifteen years," said the Admiral. "How
can I ask him to have learnt to respect age, if I in sixty years
have not learnt to respect youth?"

And with the last word he drew up his head. It was quite true that there were men who would have died for him when he stood up and spoke like that.

In the glow of momentary feeling, however, the Admiral had again forgotten the box: and the Duke had to remind him of it. Lest it should slip his mind again, he resolved to open it then and there. First, of course, he retired to his cabin and put on his State uniform. Then he assembled the whole ship's company. The proceedings were opened with prayer and the reading of the Mutiny Act and the Navy Regulations. The Admiral then delivered an address on the subject of boxes, ancient and modern—the Box in Christian and Pagan Art—Boxes of All Nations—The Influence of Democracy on the Box—Are Boxes Necessary?—and " The Box of the Future." Then in an earnest voice he declared that the supreme moment of their lives had come: a moment of importance, perhaps of danger. He drew his sword and said he hoped they were all armed.

The Professor levelled his gun at the box ready to fire at a moment's notice. The Crew dragged from his pockets, first a shower of Penny Dreadfuls and then a pistol with caps. " Lead on," he said hoarsely. " We foller yer to death."

The Duke, not having any weapon to hand, ran up the ship's gun from the porthole and jumped astride it, patting it and addressing it playfully in equine phraseology.

There was an intense silence, in which they could hear the water slapping against the sides of the yacht.

Then the Admiral said solemnly: " I declare this box open," and lifted the lid.

And out of the box rose a very, very tall thin man to his full height, till he looked down on all of them.

## LES BOILEAUX DE CASTELNAU

This poem was made for Miss Boileau, before her marriage to G.K.C.'s great friend E. C. Bentley. Her own branch of the family had been in England since the Huguenot emigration, but had kept up relations with the branch which remained in France. The family traces its records back to Etienne Boileau, who was Grand Provost of Paris in 1250; there is a tradition that among the many malefactors he hanged was his own godson. His son went on the 8th Crusade with St. Louis and died in the Holy Land. In the Jena campaign one of the family, an émigré, was with the Germans.

# LES BOILEAUX DE CASTELNAU

Provost B. his godson named
Habbukuk Zerubbabel
Then, by hanging him at once
Saved him further troub-b-ble.

This one went to the Cruzades
Matched against the Saracen
You can tell me which you think
Lost by the comparison.

Here's another: Crecy made
Him and the Black Prince
    acquainted
Short of ink, I've made the
    Prince
Not so black as he is painted.

To the Count they brought
    a Church
Which he quite declined to
    swallow;
" Swallow " is an English
    word
Do you think it rhymes
    with Boileau?

# LES BOILEAUX DE CASTELNAU

Here we see his little brother
Guardian of the Reformation
At the age of one, said " Boo Hoo !
Nasty transubstantiation."

Exile in the Austrian armies
Of whose legs I've shown
  a part
After Jena he spoke kindly
To Napoleon Buonaparte.

Ink will not express my meaning,
If I worked in pastel now
I could blue the blood of Gaston
De Boileau de Castelnau.

## LES BOILEAUX DE CASTELNAU

I had drawn the English Boileaux
All the ladies that they lend us
But that picture lies in haste
Buried. It was too tremendous.

# THE TWO TAVERNS

In the country of Old King Cole, the founder of the Colchester Oyster Feast, and therefore a distinguished diner-out, there were two partners who owned an inn called The Sun and Moon. One of them called Giles was rather loud and boastful, and the other called Miles rather silent and sarcastic; so that they soon quarrelled and set up opposition signs. That of Giles was called optimistically The Rising Sun, and that of Miles more modestly The Half Moon. There had been some dispute about the one barrel of sound wine they possessed; but at last it was drawn off into two smaller barrels in exactly equal quantities. It so happened that King Cole, with his celebrated Violin Orchestra and all his royal retinue, came riding from Colchester to the little village of London. He came first to the inn of The Rising Sun, with its beautiful groves of bushes festooned with coloured light forming the legend: " Rising Sun Ruby Wine is the Best." Mr. Giles received the monarch with prostrations of hospitality, and took occasion to observe that the Ruby Wine sold at his establishment was the Best Wine in the World. And indeed the potentate had occasion to note that a similar opinion was inscribed on the flag flying from the turret, on the large blue bow decorating the dog, and that even the sardines and other *hors d'œuvres* were arranged in patterns expressive of the same thought. When therefore the exuberant Giles had broken out for the sixth and seventh time into cries of admiring anticipation, touching the wine he intended to serve, the King, familiar by this time with the sentiment, suggested with some sharpness that the wine should be produced. His annoyance must be his excuse for the curious perversity which led him, even when the wine was produced, to say that he did not think so much of it after all. It must be remembered that he was a gentleman of the old school.

Leaving The Rising Sun, he resolved to push on to London, as there was evidently no other first-class hotel on the road; nothing but a shabby and unpretentious tavern called The Half Moon. At this, however, he consented to pause for a moment, his thirst having been greatly increased by the curious cookery of the superior hostel. " I am afraid," said Miles, the melancholy innkeeper, with an air of depression, " that there is really nothing in the house that is in the least fit to be offered to Your Majesty. We have a little cheap wine, but I fear you will think it the worst wine you ever drank in your life."

" Not at all, not at all," said the King breezily. " I assure you I know how to rough it."

And he proceeded to give Miles a somewhat misleading account of all he had gone through in his campaigns against the King of Chelmsford. And when the wine was served to him, he drank it with quite a roistering gesture and banged the goblet on the table, crying: " Blessed St. Julian, what uncommonly decent drink one can get in these little out-of-the-way places! Really, this stuff is quite excellent! I have indeed fallen on my feet."

This was not quite a correct figure of speech; he went on drinking the wine, and even attempted to dance with the village maidens; but it was not always on his feet that he fell.

# TAGTUG AND THE TREE OF KNOWLEDGE

A SENSE of stupidity can easily descend on and darken the brain; and when I for one say that I do not understand this or that, I do not necessarily imply the suspicion that there is nothing to be understood. In all sincerity, or stupidity, there are many of my own affairs that I do not understand.

The other day I came upon an instance of the scholarly information which puzzles a popular intelligence. It was in a very interesting article by a learned man, Professor Sayce, on the old Babylonian or rather (it seems) Sumerian version of the story of Adam. The sentence ran thus: " The Sumerian name of the prototype and eponym of the human race was Tag-tug, or as it was usually pronounced, Uttu." Now I have no doubt there is an explanation of this; but I think an explanation is required. If I were learned enough to instruct the general reader in such things I should instruct him a little more. If I had to say that my family name was Chesterton, pronounced Ububboo, I should have a sense that some further enquiries might be made. If I had to introduce a man by the name of Smith, and to assure everybody that it was pronounced Brown, I should anticipate a certain faint surprise and curiosity following the communication. I should be moved either to linger on the para-dox or to leave it out; but I do not doubt that Professor Sayce mentioned it thus casually because the fact is connected with other facts, with which he is quite familiar. But the fact for the ordinary reader, without any further explanation, savours a little too much of that American philologist who complained that we spell a word b,e,a,u,c,h,a,m,p, and call it Chumley. But the mystification of the mere outsider goes beyond the superficial wonder about why a man with a fine firm expressive name like Tagtug should have consented to be addressed by so sentimental a pet name as Uttu. There is also the problem involved in the very antiquity and obscurity of the subject. How can Professor Sayce be so exceedingly certain about how people who lived before the Babylonians *pronounced* a word, as distinct from how they wrote it? Has he wandered about among the prehistoric Sumerians, forlornly and fruitlessly calling out " Tagtug," to find their faces light up at last with recognition, when it occurred to him to pronounce it " Uttu? " When the archaeologist found, in the ruins of Nippur, the cuneiform tablet simply and conspicuously inscribed " Tagtug," what echoes of old Sumerian conversation still lingered in those ruins, faintly repeating " Uttu," as with ghostly voices, like horns of elfland faintly blowing? I repeat that I readily believe there is an answer to these questions; I readily believe that the Professor is right. But I am not writing to point out that the Professor is wrong; but rather to point out that the modern reader is wrong, when he supposes that his own scientific reading is based on reason, or even consists of statements in themselves reasonable. There are few of the things called the mysteries of religion, that I myself find so mystifying as that single sentence. There are few of the things controversially cited as the contradictions of Scripture that I find so inherently contradictory. Now Professor Sayce himself writes, at the beginning of his article, as if all our views of Scriptural texts, and even of religious mysteries, had been revolutionised and rationalised by this very type of information. " Science," he says, " has obliged us to change our ideas not only of the age and origin of man himself, but also of the origin of evil and of such theological problems as the consciousness of sin. This silent revolution of ideas has been assisted by the discovery and decipherment of the ancient records of the Nearer East." In short, our attitude to our own sin is altered by the discovery that the Sumerians called Adam, Tagtug; when clarified and simplified by the further discovery that they called Tagtug, Uttu. I do not know how others feel after this exposition and enlightenment; but in my own private psychology " such theological problems as the consciousness of sin " stick pretty much where they were.

For my part, I do not think that poor old Tagtug, let alone Adam, can be dismissed so easily. If the immemorial civilisation of the Near East, so old that it seems always to have been civilised, like the camel, has a tradition that the first men began to fall away from some high standard set for them from the start, I think that tradition is truer to history, as well as philosophy, than most of the half-educated and tenth-rate talk about evolution. If successive cults and cultures, one older than another, all lead back to one idea that man held happiness on a condition, and is unhappy through breaking that condition, I think they lead a long way nearer the truth of human psychology than the little bustling journeys of popular science. What in such stories is symbolic, what sacred, what beyond contemporary comprehension I do not know; nor has any theologian yet asked me to accept on faith the fact that Adam was pronounced Bingo. Professor Sayce tells us that the Babylonian story mentions more than one tree (eight, I think); but I think he cannot see the truth for the trees. He tells us that in the Babylonian version, as distinct from the Hebrew one, the Flood was coincident with the Fall as well as consequent on the Fall. But I find it much more interesting that they agree about why it came, than that they differ about when it came. In the abstract, and as a matter of personal taste, therefore, Tagtug is good enough for me. I think this ancient and mysteriously suggestive story a very suitable starting place for that real evolution that ends in the best practical morality that I know. I should be quite content, if necessary, to say that in Tagtug all died, so long as I could still say that in Christ all were made alive. But Tagtug himself, even when pronounced Uttu, is perhaps a little lacking in all this later and more living historical justification. He is not what you might call a name to conjure with now, however you pronounce him. And of the two versions of an exceedingly tenable tradition, I may be pardoned for adhering to the one which is not only true as a poem, but has in a sense come true as a prophecy.

But whether or no I am right in accepting such mystical assumptions, my point here is that fashionable scientific culture makes assumptions every bit as mystical; and states them (as in the case of Uttu) in language very much more mystifying. Whatever may be said about the Sumerian or Semitic story of the origin of man, there is not much more real logic or real evidence in the version of the origin of man now taught to thousands of people under the title of science. Mr. Wells has not got so far as man in his history of man; but his publisher adorned the cover of the first issue with a picture of primitive man as now conceived. In so far as primitive man is a man, he is more or less modelled on a butler having a bath; but he is made primitive by being flattened and brutalised so as to look like a frog. There is the same scientific evidence for this picture as there is for the godlike and golden-haired Adam of Paradise Lost. But I know that multitudes, seeing that picture, will think it is science and the other only poetry. For the rest, many theories of evolution have appeared and have collapsed, as the whole scientific theory of the cosmic basis is said to have collapsed. And if I were writing a human history professedly concrete and outside controversy, I should not begin on any disputed and dissolving Darwinian hypothesis; any more than I should begin with Tagtug and his eight trees, or Adam and his two trees. I should say that human civilisation was too old to test even its own oldest traditions; and that the wisest were doubtful about the origin of man, as about the origin of matter. In short, I should be an agnostic; a thing almost unknown nowadays. And I should add that outside this mystery there are two things: there is faith and there is fancy. The former refers to some religion; and the latter produces what the Victorian poet called, with unconscious irony, the fairy-tales of science.

Mrs Chesterton's Donkeys
in waiting

# BALLADE OF THE TEA-POT

SALT pork was sweet to Nelson's salted tar;
Russians like train-oil tipped out of a can;
Petrol appears to please a motor-car,
And potted greens a vegetarian.
When the long lines of earnest brows I scan
Only one gastric certainty I see;
In chapels chill and artists' parlours wan,
It is not well for men to live on tea.

I saw a man in wool who spoke on War.
Peculiar ladies clapped when he began.
He dared in Dulwich to defy the Czar.
He called the King " our greatest Gentleman."
He said " The flags of honour do but fan
Man's prehistoric animality."
But oh ! Dan Chaucer—oh Dan—Dan—Dan,
It is not well for men to live on tea.

Be good, sweet maid; and follow that strong star
Of sanity that lights our labouring clan;
Such things as thieving and blackmail I bar,
And piracy I positively ban.
Avoid assassination, if you can,
Don't be a slave to anthropophagy;
It is not well for men to feed on man,
It is not well for men to live on tea.

### ENVOI

Prince, here's that everlasting Lady Ann,
Let's get our coats and cut our sticks and flee;
Come round the corner to the " Pig and Swan,"
It is not well for men to live on tea.

# IMMORTAL IDIOTS:—3.

## CHARLES. I —
## or, GOING OFF HIS HEAD.

# THE PROFESSOR AND THE COOK

## I

THE long friendship between the Professor and the Cook began with the Cook throwing a huge iron pot over the Professor, but for which Gaelic gesture the Professor would have blown the Cook's brains out. Mutual esteem, and even affection, founded on this incident may perhaps allow of a little further elucidation.

The Cook had been shipwrecked on a desert island, on his way from America, where he had been a famous hotel *chef*, to France, where he aspired to be a small peasant. He floated ashore in a hollow pot like a fish-kettle; and as Robinson Crusoe took two swords from the wreck, the Cook managed to carry away two immense carving-knives as long as cutlasses; with which to defend himself against the sharks. He was thus fully equipped to carve the joint, if there had been anything to carve; just as he was profession-ally competent to cook the dinner, if there had been anything to cook.

It was at this moment, fortunately, that the Professor came out of the woods, looking rather like a wild man of the woods, though still decorated with a decayed top-hat and carrying a long gun of very curious shape. What was better, he was dragging behind him the remains of a large stag.

" I've taken a slap-up photograph," said the Professor with an American accent. " I've got a just lovely photo of the stag."

" It appears more pleasing," replied the Cook, " that you have got the stag."

" Why, see here," observed the other, " it looks like you hadn't heard of the Double Action Photogun, a little invention of my own.

"My job was scientific exploration, with snaps of big game shooting; and I guess you know the old-fashioned fuss there used to be for that; rows of old tripod cameras stuck around to click when the shot came. Well, my little machine clicks and shoots in one action; so I got a dandy lot of plates; lions leaping in their last instant and elephants rolling like earthquakes. Wal, it was a great stunt, and if I hadn't been a bit absent-minded . . . you see I was introduced to all the Crowned Heads and the judges and rulers of the land, as the Bible says; and being a newspaper man, I nat'rally wanted to snap them. At the end of each interview with a judge or politician or what not, I just photographed him; and it was a good photograph, only when I developed it I found he was sort of dead, or dying in agonies all round the apartment. Somehow I hadn't anticipated this; but I found I'd made a pretty large clearance of the best and brightest men in the state. When you have a double action like that, you're thinking sometimes of one thing and sometimes another. I had a plate of a Prime Minister leaping into the air that was just lovely; but it hadn't been quite what I intended. So I've had to take refuge in this little island."

" I can well comprehend that, me," replied the Cook. " One pursued you I imagine; Justice was on your track, despite your blameless intentions. Perhaps the People also. Is not that what you call a lynch ? "

" Not exactly," replied the Professor absent-mindedly. " When the people found what I'd done, my popularity got to be simply impossible. They wanted to make me Dictator; and I'm told some of the more elementary tribes were ready to worship me as a god."

## THE PROFESSOR AND THE COOK

The Cook stared; but the Professor, whose chief characteristic seemed to be absence of mind, was already gazing in dreamy abstraction at his companion.

"You'd make some fine figure for the film," said the Professor, "standing there stuck with two great knives, like a pirate. I've half a mind to . . ."

And the Professor, whose characteristic was absence of mind, vaguely lifted his instrument. But the Cook, whose characteristic was presence of mind, hurled the huge pot over his head, covering him completely from view, till he had a few moments of meditation in which to realise his error.

## II

The Professor and the Cook (cast together on their desert island) became bosom friends. The next occasion on which they encountered each other with any really violent bodily assault and battery, not only ended but even began in a glow of friendship.

The Professor was explaining the properties of his famous Photogun, which killed any living creature and took its portrait by the same simple mechanical action; and was praising, in his simple way, the superiority of such machinery over older weapons: such as those of the Cook, who was girt about with two carving knives looking nearly as big as sabres. The Professor proudly recounted how, armed with this gun alone, he had defied and defeated a whole tribe of wild dervishes in the desert. The fanatics were indifferent to being shot, but on learning that they were also to be photographed, their Moslem scruples against portraiture led them to surrender in thousands.

"That will show," said the Professor, "what I owe to modern science and its instrument."

# THE PROFESSOR AND THE COOK

"It seems to me," replied the Cook, "that you owe it not to modern science but to ancient superstition. Had they not obligingly provided the commandment, it were vain for you to provide the camera. Besides, I have a doubt about this scientific superiority of fire-arms, founded on an incident still generally narrated (though mostly, I admit, to persons under six years old) in my own beautiful Burgundian valley."

"Do you mean that it happened to you?" asked the Professor suspiciously.

"I have no doubt it did," replied the Cook dispassionately, "but it must have happened at so early an age that I cannot vouch for it except as a tradition. It concerned a worthy youth who had a wicked uncle called Le Docteur Simon; this docteur had a very queer shaped hat and still more peculiar whiskers; he had very long coat tails and carried a very long gun. On the other hand he had rather short trousers and was followed by an unnaturally spotted dog. You have seen him often in the nursery books of the first year of the nineteenth century. His nephew, conceiving a natural dislike of his wickedness and his whiskers, attempted to run away; but the wicked Doctor said in a dreadful voice that sounded through the dark but neat plantation, 'You will not escape; because I have the Longest Gun in the World; and you will see it pointed at you everywhere.' And sure enough, though he fled first to the end of the garden, and then to the end of the park, and then beyond the forest, he always saw the muzzle and bore of that titanic telescopic gun looking at him like a single sinister eye."

The Cook was telling the nursery story in a dreamy voice that seemed to drift them away from their sub-tropical islet to the dim orchards and dank gardens of home, the tufted trees like brooms and the tumbling clouds; then he sat up suddenly and said in a business-like tone, " So he prayed to St. Nicholas, who naturally appeared to him in a vision and offered him advice which appeared paradoxical and even exasperating. ' Do not run away from your enemy; always run towards him,' said the Saint and vanished with irritating abruptness, in a blaze of glory. But it was perfectly true. When the boy had once dodged past the muzzle of the gun, the Doctor could only wave it about in wild efforts to recover the range; and was at length forced actually to run away from the little boy as fast as his legs could carry him, in the desperate hope of shortening his unduly elongated weapon. The boy, who had armed himself with a carving knife (being a youth of superior intelligence) had the felicity of chasing his venerable but unpleasant relative over hill and dale for miles, merely because the latter had neglected to provide himself with anything short enough for a combat at close quarters. This story has not only an elegant woodcut for a tailpiece, but also a moral; which is, ' The eyes of a fool are in the ends of the earth.' "

" I do not believe it," said the Professor, and leapt up, gun in hand, in purely intellectual excitement. And so it began.

### III

The desert island on which the Professor and the Cook had been shipwrecked was once more a scene of personal conflict between those devoted and affectionate friends. The causes that led up to it, however, were highly intellectual and not without their interest to a curious mind.

The Professor was the most mild and amiable of men; he had killed a good many people by his own account, but quite inadvertently, in attempting to photograph them with his celebrated Photogun. But he was not without a dash of American humour and bragging; and it may be that he exaggerated his bag. But the Professor had what every Professor has. He had a Feud; a hobby that was a hatred; a standing quarrel in connection with his Subject. His Subject was the Great Sea Serpent; its non-existence; and especially the degraded quackery of another Professor who thought it might exist. So it was quite an awkward and delicate situation when the Cook, pacing the shore of the desert island, distinctly saw the Great Sea Serpent approaching, as long as a marine parade and with a head as high as a church spire. The Cook was a Frenchman, with a round head, a square body and a realism not to be rocked by earthquakes; but he felt quite nervous about breaking the Sea Serpent to the more delicate mind of his friend. At that moment the friend came out of the hut with his Photogun and instantly and almost automatically photographed the monster and shot it dead. This, the Cook reflected, was unfortunate; a live Sea Serpent might have dived and disappeared and would then of course have been a hallucination. But a dead Sea Serpent washed up on the shore and decaying for months was less easy to explain away. He watched his friend as the latter walked moodily round the monstrous corpse, which had rolled inshore and lay in writhing coils as large as round Roman arches. At length he was puzzled to see the Professor stretch his arms, stamp a little with his feet, and open his mouth very wide. He was yawning.

" I wish I could wake up," he said. " It is quite obvious by all scientific processes of thought that this is a nightmare. My arguments disproving this fabulous creature were quite conclusive. The only deduction is a dream."

" But see," said the Cook, " let us be logical. If you are only dreaming that you see the Serpent, so also you are only dreaming that you had the scientific argument. If one is an illusion, why not the other. But if your argument is an illusion, the Serpent may not be an illusion. And so we go on."

"I wish to wake up," repeated the Professor firmly. "Will you kindly stab me with one of those large carving knives you carry. As they are entirely subjective carving knives the depth of the stab will be immaterial."

Strange to say, his friend still hesitated; and the Professor snatched one of the big blades and brandished it quite excitedly.

"Now I come to think of it," he cried, "I may very well kill you, as you are only a dream. In real life I have a warm attachment for you, or rather your prototype; but my remorse for murdering you will probably wake me up to enjoy your society at breakfast."

And with these words he rushed upon his friend, slashing wildly, and it is fortunate that the Frenchman was expert in the national art of fencing and could parry the blows. At last the Cook was forced to deliver that prick in the wrist which has ended many duels. The Professor dropped his weapon and seemed really to wake up. For an instant he stood rigid with despair; then he gave a great shout.

"I had forgotten! Converging proof! How can science be certain without confirmation by converging proof! I have not yet developed the photograph. Until that is done, the evidence cannot be considered final."

And jumping over the end of the Great Sea Serpent's tail, which ran like a low wall along the sand, he plunged into the hut and brought out his chemicals, to see whether the creature was discernible in the photograph.

When the Professor on the desert island really saw the Sea Serpent recorded not only on the faulty human retina but the faultless photographic plate, he was struck down by delirium and lay raving for weeks on end. He did so from a sense of duty, delirium being the only scientific excuse for seeing snakes.

His friend the Cook waited on him with personal affection and professional skill; indeed the skill was much needed, for the winter store of food consisted entirely of the dead Sea Serpent, which the Cook had to serve up a slice at a time, but so ingeniously disguised with herbs and vegetable sauces as to conceal the very existence of the unmentionable reptile. And as the Cook had been taught (probably by Jesuits) the infamous doctrine that it is sometimes permissible to deceive the sick or the insane, he rather prided himself on the variety of his deceptions. He did not lie weakly and evasively, like a Puritan grocer looking down his nose. He lied joyously, radiantly, creatively, like a Latin; and insinuated into the description of each dish some new explanation that might soothe the nightmare of his friend.

Thus he began by saying lightly that the succession of somewhat similar slices came from the neck of a giraffe. On his patient detecting a faintly salt savour rare in giraffes he hastened to explain that it was a variety called the water-giraffe; and happily added that a giraffe's neck coming out of the water might easily have been taken for a Sea Serpent. Warming to his work, he said next day that the marine savour was due to the seasoning coming from that remarkable vegetation known as the Igesitzalla Plant.

" Not only," said the Cook gravely, " does it tower into tall trees on this island, but its roots have the remarkable property of piercing their way to the sea, where they wave about like tentacles and feed on fishes, which they kill by lifting them out of their native element high into the air. Such a tentacle, ending with the goggling head of a fish, might easily have deceived your eye."

"True," said the Professor faintly. "True. Why did I never think of so simple an explanation?"

"The bird I have served up to-day," said the Cook brightly, at the next meal, "is called by the natives of these parts the Noendova Lark. The name in the native tongue is said to be derived from the fact that these birds swim in a chain, with the tail of each held securely in the bill of the one behind. When the leader rises to fly, the whole chain rises after him into the air; had you observed it at that moment, it might well have had the appearance of a long reptile."

"Yes," said the Professor quite eagerly, "perhaps the creatures are cannibalistic; each attempting to devour the other."

"And each being a little too large to be devoured," said the Cook. "That is no doubt the rational explanation. Indeed I believe the bird is also known as the Morthanucan Swallow."

"It is as I suspected," said the Professor faintly but firmly. "I knew there was a perfectly rational explanation."

It was perhaps fortunate that by the time the Professor had really recovered, and could walk on wavering legs outside the hut, they had at last eaten their way through the Sea Serpent. The Professor's eye swept the circle of blue sea and green island without encountering any offence.

"About that curious experience of ours," he said, coughing slightly, "I am prepared to admit there was a psychological element; a sort of double hallucination. But I am sure it was wholly subjective. I mean it was an inner experience; it was within ourselves."

"It is now," said the Cook.

# GIRL GUIDES

WHEN Cleopatra was made a Guide,
She let her militant duties slide,
And when her prattle had lost the battle
Tactfully tickled a snake and died.

When Boadicea was made a Guide,
Her visage the vividest blue was dyed;
So the coat was made of a similar shade
And she travelled on wheels with the spokes outside.

When Lady Godiva was made a Guide,
The uniform had to be simplified,
But the rates were high, and she was not shy,
And they say it was only the horse that shied.

When Bloody Mary was made a Guide,
She told the people that when she died
Topographical notes on her views and her votes
If they took her to bits would be found inside.

When Queen Victoria was made a Guide,
She never excelled on the giant stride,
Or won a place in the obstacle race,
And historians doubt if she even tried.

When Messalina was made a Guide . . .
. . . But the trouble is that the form I've tried,
Though far from clever, might last for ever,
With hundreds and hundreds of names beside.

# WONDER AND THE WOODEN POST

BLACK night had shut in my house and garden with shutters first of slate and then of ebony; I was making my way indoors by the fiery square of the lamplit window, when I thought I saw something new sticking out of the ground, and bent over to look at it. In so doing I knocked my head against a post and saw stars; stars of the seventh heaven, stars of the secret and supreme firmament. For it did truly seem, as the slight pain lessened but before the pain had wholly passed, as if I saw written in an astral alphabet on the darkness something that I had never understood so clearly before: a truth about the mysteries and the mystics which I have half known all my life. I shall not be able to put the idea together again with the words upon this page, for these queer moods of clearness are always fugitive: but I will try. The post is still there; but the stars in the brain are fading.

When I was young I wrote a lot of little poems, mostly about the beauty and necessity of Wonder; which was a genuine feeling with me, as it is still. The power of seeing plain things and landscapes in a kind of sunlight of surprise; the power of jumping at the sight of a bird as if at a winged bullet; the power of being brought to a standstill by a tree as by the gesture of a gigantic hand; in short, the power of poetically running one's head against a post is one which varies in different people and which I can say without conceit is a part of my own human nature. It is not a power that indicates any artistic strength, still less any spiritual exaltation; men who are religious in a sense too sublime for me to conceive are equally without it. Of the pebble in the pathways of the twig on the hedge, it may truly be said that many prophets and righteous men have desired to see these things and have not seen them. It is a small and special gift, but an innocent one.

As my little poems were mostly bad poems, they attracted a certain amount of attention among modern artists and critics; I was told that I was a mystic and found myself being introduced to whole rows and rows of mystics; most of them much older and wiser than I. Of course, there were professional quacks and amateur asses among them; but not in much larger proportion than would have appeared among politicians or men of science or any other mixed convention. There was the long-faced, elderly man, who said, in a deep bass voice like distant thunder: " What we want is Love"; which was true enough, if to want means to lack. There was the little, radiant man, who radiated all his fingers outwards and cried: " Heaven is here! It is now! " as if he were selling something, as he probably was. There was the chirpy little man who took one confidentially into a corner and said quietly: " There is no true difference between good and bad, false and true; they are alike leading us upwards." He was easily disposed of; merely by asking, if there was no difference between good and bad, what was the difference between up and down? But it would be gravely and grossly unjust to suggest that any of these represented the modern mystics whose acquaintance I made. I met many men whom history and literature will rightly remember. I met the man who was and is by far the greatest poet who has written in English for decades. For I will not call Mr. Yeats an English poet; I will only say that I should be sorry to see him translated into any other language. I met a man like

# WONDER AND THE WOODEN POST

Mr. Herbert Burrows who, almost alone among men in my knowledge, contrived to combine an Oriental and impersonal religion with that hard fighting and hot magnanimity which we in the west mean when we are speaking of a man. There were great poets and great fighters, then, among these modern mystics whom I met; and their genius and sincerity, as well as their mysticism, led me to conclude that they were quite right. And yet there was something inside me telling me, with what I can only call a stifled scream, that they were quite wrong. It was the same for that matter with my early economic opinions. I was a Socialist in my youth; because the attack on Socialism, as then conducted, left a man no choice except to be a Socialist or a scoundrel. But, even then, long before I ceased to be a Socialist, long before I heard of peasant ownership or any other escape from our present disgrace, I had felt by a sort of tug in my bones that the Fabians and the Marxians were pulling the world one way when I wanted it to go the other. So I felt about great mystics like Mr. Yeats; about sane theosophists like Mr. Burrows. I felt, not merely that their mysticism was in flat contradiction to mine—more even than materialism. I went on feeling this; it took me a long time to give it even an obscure expression. I never found a really vivid expression until I knocked my head against the post. The expression that leapt to my lips then, I am (as I say) forgetting slowly.

Now what I found finally about our contemporary mystics was this. When they said that a wooden post was wonderful (a point on which we are all agreed, I hope) they meant that they could make something wonderful out of it by thinking about it. "Dream; there is no truth," said Mr. Yeats, "but in your own heart." The modern mystic looked for the post, not outside in the garden, but inside, in the mirror of his mind. But the mind of the modern mystic, like a dandy's dressing-room, was entirely made of mirrors. Thus glass repeated glass like doors opening inwards for ever; till one could hardly see that inmost chamber of unreality where the post made its last appearance. And as the mirrors of the modern mystic's mind are most of them curved and many of them cracked, the post in its ultimate reflection looked like all sorts of things; a waterspout, the tree of knowledge, the sea-serpent standing upright, a twisted column of the new natural architecture, and so on. Hence we have Picasso and a million puerilities. But I was never interested in mirrors; that is, I was never primarily interested in my own reflection—or reflections. I am interested in wooden posts, which do startle me like miracles. I am interested in the post that stands waiting outside my door, to hit me over the head, like a giant's club in a fairy tale. All my mental doors open outwards into a world I have not made. My last door of liberty opens upon a world of sun and solid things, of objective adventures. The post in the garden; the thing I could neither create nor expect: strong plain daylight on stiff upstanding wood: it is the Lord's doing, and it is marvellous in our eyes.

When the modern mystics said they liked to see a post, they meant they liked to imagine it. They were better poets than I; and they imagined it as soon as they saw it. Now I might see a post long before I had imagined it—and (as I have already described) I might feel it before I saw it. To me the post is wonderful because it is *there*; there whether I like it or not. I was struck silly by a post, but if I were struck blind by a thunderbolt, the post would still be there; the substance of things not seen. For the amazing thing about the universe is that it exists; not that we can discuss its existence. All real spirituality is a testimony to this world as much as the other: the material universe does exist. The Cosmos still quivers to its topmost star from that great kick that Dr. Johnson gave the stone when he defied Berkeley. The kick was not philosophy—but it was religion.

Now the mystics around me had not this lively faith that things are fantasies because they are facts. They wanted, as all magicians did, " to control the elements "; to *be* the Cosmos. They wished the stars to be their omnipresent eyes and winds their long wild tongues unrolled; and therefore they favoured twilight, and all the dim and borderland mediums in which one thing melts into another—in which a man can be as large as Nature and (what is worse) as impersonal as Nature. But I never was properly impressed with the mystery of twilight, but rather with the riddle of daylight, as huge and staring as the sphinx. I felt it in big bare buildings against a blue sky, high houses gutted or still empty, great blank walls washed with warm light as with a monstrous brush. One seemed to have come to the back of everything. And everything had that strange and high indifference that belongs only to things that are. . . You see I have not said what I meant: but if you admit that my head and the post were equally wonderful, I give you leave to say they were equally wooden.

DIOGENES TEACHES ALEXANDER PATIENCE

# A BALLADE OF DEAD MEN

COME, let us sit upon the grass
And tell sad tales of human ill:
How Bacon was a silly ass
Who caught a Chicken and a Chill;
And Charles the First, who made his will
But managed to mislay his head;
And Brown, who read the works of Mill,
Who is unfortunately dead.

Queen Bess, who swore upon the Mass
How many Catholics she'd kill;
Our glorious Marlborough, who, alas !
Could not be trusted near the till;
Chatham, who'd set the world a-thrill
And quite abruptly go to bed;
And Tims, who took the " Deathless " Pill,
Who is unfortunately dead.

Tales cling but fade; and falls the glass
That Rosamunda failed to spill;
Faint rails the fragrance of the Lass
Along the tiles of Richmond Hill:
But Genesis is printed still,
And Homer's verses still are read—
A writer of no little skill
Who is unfortunately dead.

# A BALLADE OF DEAD MEN

## Envoi

Prince, pearls and diamonds, take your fill;
Don't mind if they are splashed with red:
I got them from my poor Aunt Jill,
Who is unfortunately dead.

A True Victorian cuts a disreputable author ——.

# THE TAMING OF THE NIGHTMARE

LITTLE JACK HORNER sat in the corner—so far the traditional surroundings of the nursery hero correspond with those in which we find him for the purposes of the story, but there being no Christmas pie in the neighbourhood, he was unable to give vent to the joyful, if somewhat egotistical, sentiment which is recorded of him elsewhere. He sat in a corner, under the window, listening to the weird moaning of the night-wind without, now tapping at the door like a wayfarer, now whistling in the chimney like a sweep, now seeming to wander, darkly muttering, like some mysterious wild thing in the copse around the cottage, now rushing like some vast monster over the roof with a hoarse roar rising to a piping shriek as it died away. Then came violent rattling at the window above him, which grew louder and fiercer till Jack expected the glass to fly to pieces, and the next moment he fancied he could hear a hoarse voice, muffled by coming through the window say, " Let me in, why can't you let me in." The vague, mystified awe that he had felt at the thousand suggestive voices of the wind changed into weird terror, and he cowered beneath the window striving not to look round, but compelled to turn by the horrible fascination of the presence of something behind him. He turned, threw open the window and looked out into the night. At first he could see nothing but the darkness, but the next moment he made out a broad, weird, goblin face with goggle eyes and a broad, queer hat, peering in through the window. " You're wanted," said the creature who appeared to be some species of watchman, in a muffled voice. "What for, Sir," gasped Jack faintly. "You," said the goblin, "are commissioned by the local Board of Good Fairies to find the Mare's Nest. The Grey Mare, who built her nest in the suburbs of Creation, where people don't so much mind what they do, has a large family, all mares

and all grey, except one, the youngest, who is as black as night, and as weird. And she is called the Nightmare. Her you must catch and tame and saddle and bridle, and she is the only steed you shall ever ride."

"And who are you, Sir," asked the boy in some wonder.

"I am the Wind," answered the Spirit. "I fill the ears of men with a thousand voices, but never before have mortal eyes seen me. I go where I list and sing what song I please. I alone can guide you to the land of the Mare's Nest. Catch hold of my cloak."

A deep, solemn fear at his heart made Jack lay hold of the mantle obediently, the Wind turned with a whistle, and the next moment Jack was jerked bodily out of the window and carried away far over the house-tops under the midnight sky, hanging on behind to the vast, wild coat-tails of the guide. They left the city, with its roofs and chimney-pots, behind, and passed on over fields and lanes, over glens and ravines, on over dim, barren wildernesses. For hours they flew, leaving the bats and owls behind, till they came to a low, lonely wall, beside which there was a dilapidated notice board, looking the other way, stating that trespassers would be prosecuted, by order of somebody, no one quite knew who.

And beyond the wall there appeared to be nothing but mist and moonshine. And the Wind turned and said gravely, " Can't go any farther, Sir, not my beat. But that's your way." And jerking his large head in the direction of the mysterious land over the wall, he moved away. And Jack clambered over the wall and entered the borderland of Creation. Before he had gone far he came to a drop in the barren moors, which showed him the broad pale face of the moon, ten times as large as usual, and dark against it the lank melancholy figure of what looked like an overgrown calf. He came nearer, and had to violently pull the large animal's tail before he consented to take the least notice of his presence. Then he slowly swung round, a large, pale, overgrown head, with round rolling eyes, and looked abstractedly at the wayfarer. " Can you tell me, where is the Mare's Nest ? " asked Jack.

The Calf eyed him wistfully for a moment, and then replied in a melancholy voice, with what appeared to be an impromptu rhyme of doubtful relevancy !

" Oh, my limbs are very feeble,
My head is very big,
My ears are round, O do not, pray
Mistake me for a pig."

"Well, who wants to?" said the exasperated Horner. "I only want to be directed."

The Calf lifted his eyes to the moon a moment and then sang plaintively.

> "This Calf was the Mooncalf, the Cow was the Moon,
> She died from effects of a popular tune,
> And now in her glory she shines in the sky;
> Oh, never had Calf such a mother as I."

And so sweet and pathetic for the moment was the upward look of the poor monster that Jack was quite touched and forgot his own business and just stroked the lean ribs of the Mooncalf. And after a long pause there rose again from the creature the wild queer songs of worship.

> "I forget all the creatures that taunt and despise,
> When through the dark night-mists my mother doth rise,
> She is tender and kind and she shines the night long
> On her lunatic child as he sings her his song.
> I was dropped on the dim earth to wander alone,
> And save this pale monster no child she hath known
> Without like on the earth, without sister or brother
> I sit here and sing to my mystical mother."

And he sat there and sang for the remainder of the interview and as Jack, slowly and almost reluctantly, made his way onward over the dark moors, he could still hear the plaintive songs of the poetic Mooncalf rising, a solitary hum upon that gloomy waste, to the white moon overhead.

And he went on until he came to what appeared to be a low garden wall, along which he ran until he came to where it sloped down a little to a small wooden gate, and looking through he saw a strange spectacle. The whole of the sloping downs beyond, as far almost as to the horizon, were apparently cultivated like a gigantic kitchen garden, on which grew enormous turnips, almost entirely above ground, with round goblin eyes, that glimmered in ranks like gas-lamps lining all the slopes under the night-sky. And above these armies of goblin turnips on the hill was a little thatched cottage, apparently belonging to the Gardener. Presently, as he stood there, staring at this singular back-garden, one or two of the round, glowing eyes suddenly went out, and a dull, gibbering moan came out of the darkness. The next moment the door of the cottage opened and a tall, bony figure with a turned down broad

hat and a demoniac-looking rake came out of the cottage and, rolling round a pair of eyes as bright and glowing as theirs, requested to know what was the matter.

"The light's gone out, oh, the light's gone out," moaned the turnips again. The Gardener retired again into the house, and came out again with a short candle burning in each hand. He made his way through the lines of turnips. Opening a door in the back of their heads, he placed the light inside, and instantly two pairs of eyes glared out as fiercely as ever. Back came the Gardener, taking half a mile at a stride over the wide downs of his kitchen-garden, and as he came back he saw Jack, who was peeping through the wooden paling.

"Who are you," he roared with a voice like thunder.

"I am Jack Horner," replied that intrepid individual.

The nursery rhymes had not formed a part of the Gardener's course of reading, so he knitted his brow and bellowed. "Do you know where you are?

"Well, not altogether," replied the boy. "Where am I?"

"This," replied the tall Gardener, "is the garden of the turnip-ghosts. They are grown and sent to Covent Garden every morning. They have a great sale among people of your race, but none of your race ever came here before, or shall again. Come, you won't object to being buried up to the neck and having a candle put inside your head, will you."

"Indeed, I shall object very much," replied Jack stoutly. "And what's more, I shan't do it."

"Shan't is rude," said the tall gardener, showing a row of gleaming teeth, and, making a sudden dart, he lifted Jack by the collar and dropped him inside the enclosure. Jack, however, was not to be beaten so easily, but running full tilt at the gardener

he upset him with a bang among the turnips, sending his long rake flying ten miles off. But the Giant was on his feet again in a moment, and, snatching his largest flower-pot, he hurled it so as to come down, neatly enclosing Jack underneath; but the boy kicked it to pieces and clutching the nearest missiles, two large turnips, which he tore up by the roots, he hurled them at the head of his enemy, who sent them back with additions. Then began a battle worthy of an epic. For days and nights they fought each other all over the hills, tearing up the turnips by thousands and flinging them pell-mell about the land. And at the end of a week's fighting, there was not a turnip lighted or growing in the land, but here and there a dying candle would make a dismal flame in the chaotic darkness. And the Gardener went aimlessly about the world, looking for his hat, and Jack continued his pilgrimage.

And at last he came to a strange land, where the rocks and mountain crests seemed as ragged and fantastic as the clouds of sunset, where wild and sudden lights, breaking out in nooks and clefts, were all that lit the sombre twilight of the world. And one day, as he wandered over the rocks and dales, he heard, suddenly, sounding through the darkness from over his head, a kind of long, shrill, demoniac neigh, which echoed weirdly over the lonely hills. And perched upon a hill-crest far above the dark mists, he could see the outline of what looked like a grey foal, looking down into the valley. The next moment the wild sound echoed again and it disappeared. Then he said to himself, " I am near the nest of the Grey Mare."

And after walking for a long time there came a fierce glare of light behind the hills, and he saw on the loftiest and most mysterious crest the fantastic head and mane of a great grey mare, perched in a nest like an eagle's. After a long climb he came to the base of the cliff on which the nest was perched and he could see the Grey Mare rolling her fiery eyes far over the lonely world; and scattered over the crags beneath her weird brood of mares were playing their demoniac gambols. And farthest of all, on the brink of an awful precipice, was the long black form and floating

mane of the Nightmare, the darkest and most hideous of all. And when he saw it he gave a cry and ran towards it. All the grey mares, wandering like ghosts about the slopes, eyed him doubtfully as he went past, but the Nightmare, when she saw him, gave a scream like thunder and skipped wildly down the other side of the hill, whither Jack followed her. Then began a chase in which leagues and months were covered. Now the Nightmare would be flying far ahead of him, like a startled deer, far over the level plain and moors, now, with a still more maddening agility, she would be dancing indolently a few feet in front of him, in and out among the rocks, seeming to suggest by the very tossing of her long tail her contempt for human pursuit. Sometimes she would stand on her head a few yards off and smile at him till he came near, then flash off and grin at him round the corner of a rock. But neither his failure nor her scorn could make the stubborn little boy give

180

up his appointed task, and in time he began to see the reward of his persistence.

The Nightmare began to lose her temper and try to get rid of him, thereby denoting that she no longer felt herself equal to the race, till at length, when they came to the strand of a moaning sea, close under a level face of cliffs, the Nightmare ran along at a

quick trot till she came to a round hole in the rocks, which looked ten times too small for her, gave a squirm and vanished inside. Jack began to feel that things were even getting a little, as it were, unusual, if one may say so, but he clenched his hands and crept into the hole, which only just held him, and crawled along a dark low passage, at the end of which, upon a heap of skulls and bones, sat the Nightmare with gleaming eyes and teeth, and he knew that she was at bay. But Jack, who always felt compassion at inopportune moments, was willing to make an amicable arrangement. "Why do you object to my riding on you," he asked. "I wish you no harm, but rather that we may both help each other. All things should help each other. It is the will of the Central Board."

"Mortal," replied the Nightmare, with a hideous laugh. "Dost thou not know that I am no common mare. The Nightmare am I, the child of horror, and mine is it to ride upon thee. Many myriads of thy race have I ridden and made them my slaves, oppressing them with visions." And with that her eyes flamed terribly and her nose seemed to grow longer and longer as she came towards him. The next moment they were struggling for the mastery, rolling over one another, so that now one was uppermost and now the other.

And when Jack was undermost, with the black fiend sitting grinning on his chest, strange trances fell upon him and he fancied that he was falling from heights and fleeing down interminable roads, with a strange hopelessness in everything. And when, with a mighty effort, he cast them off, and threw his enemy under him, he found himself upon a silent moor under the starlight. So, through a long night, they kept changing places, till at last, after one fierce, foaming struggle—side by side, Jack rose uppermost, and tossed back his dishevelled hair, and the Nightmare sank helpless beneath him. She appeared to have fainted, and, after what the poor lady had gone through, it was perhaps not to be wondered at.

And Jack took the big, ugly head in his lap and kissed it and guarded it in silence, till at last the Nightmare opened her eyes, now as mild as the Mooncalf's, whinnied sorrowfully and rubbed her head against him. At last the Nightmare rose and stood silent and ready and Jack sprang upon her back and they rode away. And as they went, they passed by the Mooncalf, who was sitting on a stone, singing, with his tail feebly beating time.

> " On thy poor offspring thy pale beams be given,
> Turning the dull moor to white halls of heaven,
> And in my songs, O Cow, from your memory slide off
> The painful effects of the tune that you died of.
> We sit here alone, but a joy to each other,
> The light to the child and the songs to the mother."

He feared at first lest the grisly form of the Nightmare should frighten the poor Mooncalf, as indeed it frightened everything else on his way, but fears, like every other emotion save the filial,

were unknown to the pale and lonely monstrosity. He was quite content, gazing plaintively up to the moon, and let the grim Nightmare go by as if it were the most conventional of quadrupeds. Once men had tried to domesticate the Mooncalf by taking it into the land of sunlight and decorating it with laurels, but it pined and wailed pathetically for the Moon, which was proverbially absurd. And at last it broke loose from the everyday world and wandered away again into the land of moonshine, far more happy than many people would believe.

Meanwhile Jack and his dark steed had made their way to the wall and the notice-board, and re-entered the land of the real. But before he had gone far over the hard fields and stony ways of the old world, Jack saw that the poor Nightmare was limping and stumbling lamentably, and remembered that shoes were not provided in the vicinity of which she had been an inhabitant. Leading her with all speed to the nearest town he interviewed a blacksmith, who agreed to shoe her for the usual consideration. But the curious, not to say discommoding, part of the proceeding was that the Nightmare who walked as mildly as a lamb while Jack himself was holding her, no sooner did the latter let go and the blacksmith approached her with a shoe than she gave a demoniac roar and kicked him through the roof. The apprentices and bystanders made a rush to secure the animal, but she fired out like a prize fighter, her legs appeared to have about twenty joints, from the way in which they flashed and curled about, knocking down man after man.

She appeared to thoroughly enjoy the fight, which was more than they did: her eyes glared with a lurid flame, her teeth and tongue protruded derisively, she appeared to grow more frightful every moment. None of the men dared approach her, as she

sat viciously rubbing her nose with her hoof and grinning at them.

"Aha," she said, scornfully, "worms of mortal race, would ye lift your puny iron machinery against the living machinery of infernal life. Well may ye tremble, for my shadow is in your doors, and I will eat out your hearts with terror." Just at this promising stage of affairs, Jack came quietly forward with a hammer in one hand and the shoe in the other. The moment the flaring eyes of the monster encountered his face, she moaned and bowed her head, and Jack, taking the tools into his own hand, shoed her himself and rode away. And as he passed through the streets all the people murmured and hooted, and one man incautiously got in the way, whereupon the Nightmare spurned him over the chimney pots and the rest preserved a respectful distance.

Now it so happened that the King was resolved to hold a great display of tournaments in the town, to which came all the knights and warriors of his and the neighbouring countries. And when the lists were ready under the throne and bannered galleries and canopies, there rode forth on either side, with flaming crests and snorting chargers, the mightiest tilters of the land. And third of those who entered the lists, after the Prince Valentine of Vandala, and Lord Breacan of the Lance, rode a wild-eyed bare-headed boy, on a lank, black mare, broken-kneed, with a mane and tail brushing the ground. And when the King and the spectators saw the strange newcomer they roared with laughter, until the plunging and crashing of the jousting knights drew their attention away. And all the while the broken-kneed mare and her rider stood silent. Suddenly, at the turning point of the fight, when Prince Valentine threw down his strongest opponent and rose

victorious over the thick of the fray, the strange boy shook the hair from his forehead, levelled his rude spear and whispered something to his dismal and shabby steed. The mare gave a piercing yell that made the whole company jump out of their skin, and went like a thunderbolt, so that the boy's spear smote Prince Valentine on the vizor and laid him neatly on his back.

The Prince sprang up, amid the shouts, and flew at him, sword in hand, but ere either could strike, the Nightmare, who now stood as dismal as ever, showed its frightful teeth and, biting the weapon off short, munched it up with much apparent enjoyment. The Prince retired cursing, but Breacan of the Lance, a mailed giant, with a spear like a ship's mast, galloped down upon them. The Nightmare gave a hideous grin and, shooting forward, squirmed and vanished suddenly, rider and all, between the front legs of the giant's horse, so that in another moment he was suddenly shot head over heels and rolled on the ground.

The boy rode forward to the King's throne. "Give me the prize," he cried. "I and my good steed have vanquished the victors."

The King started to his feet, and his brow was dark. "There is some sorcery," he said, "in this boy and his black jade. Secure him."

The boy laughed. "Secure me yourself, liar," he said. "While I ride my mare, you may try." He was about to turn away, but the Nightmare took matters into her own hands. With a roar like a clap of thunder she shot forward, upset throne and King and the next moment was miles away on the moors. "Come," said the boy dismounting, "since men will not receive us, we will go on our way together. Perhaps we will visit the Mooncalf again and see your mother and your brothers."

" My master," said the Nightmare, sitting down at his feet. " I have no mother nor brothers. I know no one but you, who does not shrink from me. But you are my master and I will go with you whither you will."

IMMORTAL IDIOTS.--4.

NELSON

OR, NOT ALL THERE.

# ON HOUSEHOLD GODS AND GOBLINS

SOMETIME ago I went with some children to see Maeterlinck's fine and delicate fairy play about the Blue Bird that brought everybody happiness. For some reason or other it did not bring me happiness, and even the children were not quite happy. I will not go so far as to say that the Blue Bird was a Blue Devil, but it left us in something seriously like the blues. The children were partly dissatisfied with it because it did not end with a Day of Judgment; because it was never revealed to the hero and heroine that the dog had been faithful and the cat faithless. For children are innocent and love justice; while most of us are wicked and naturally prefer mercy.

But there was something wrong about the Blue Bird, even from my more mature and corrupt point of view. There were several incidental things I did not like. I did not like the sentimental passage about the love-affair of two babes unborn; it seemed to me a piece of what may be called bad Barrie; and logically it spoilt the only meaning of the scene, which was that the babes were looking to all earthly experiences as things inconceivable. I was not convinced when the boy exclaimed, " There are no dead," for I am by no means sure that he (or the dramatist) knew what he meant by it. " I heard a voice from Heaven cry: Blessed are the dead. . . . " I do not know all that is meant in that; but I think the person who said it knew. But there was something more continuous and clinging in the whole business which left me vaguely restless. And I think the nearest to a definition was that I felt as if the poet was condescending to everything; condescending to pots and pans and birds and beasts and babies.

The one part of the business which I really felt to be original and suggestive was the animation of all the materials of the household, as if with familiar spirits; the spirit of fire, the spirit of water and the rest. And even here I felt a faint difference which moved me to an imaginary comparison. I wonder that none of our medievalists has made a Morality or allegorical play founded on the Canticle of Saint Francis, which speaks somewhat similarly of Brother Fire and Sister Water. It would be a real exercise in Gothic craftsmanship and decoration to make these symbolic figures at once stiff and fantastic. If nobody else does this I shall be driven to spoil the idea myself, as I have spoiled so many other rather good ideas in my time. But the point of the parallel at the moment is merely this: that the medieval poet does strike me as having felt about fire like a child while the modern poet felt about it like a man talking to children.

Few and simple as are the words of the older poem, it does somehow convey to me that when the poet spoke of fire as untameable and strong, he felt it as something that might conceivably be feared as well as loved. I do not think the modern poet feared the nursery fire as a child who loved it might fear it. And this elemental quality in the real primitives brought back to my mind something I have always felt about this conception, which is the really fine conception in the Blue Bird: I mean something like that which the heathens embodied in the images of the household gods. The household gods, I believe, were carved out of wood; which makes them even more like the chairs and tables.

The nomad and the anarchist accuse the domestic ideal of being merely timid and prim. But this is not because they themselves are bolder or more vigorous, but simply because they do not know it well enough to know how bold and vigorous it is. The most nomadic life to-day is not the life of the desert but of the industrial cities. It is by a very accurate accident that we talk about a Street-Arab; and the Semitic description applies to not a few gutter-snipes whose gilded chariots have raised them above the gutter. They live in clubs and hotels and are often simply ignorant, I might almost say innocent, of the ancient life of the family, and certainly of the ancient life on the farm.

When a townsman first sees these things directly and intimately, he does not despise them as dull but rather dreads them as wild, as he sometimes takes a tame cow for a wild bull. The most obvious example is the hearth which is the heart of the home. A man living in the lukewarm air of centrally-heated hotels may be said to have never seen fire. Compared to him the housewife at the fireside is an Amazon wrestling with a flaming dragon. The same moral might be drawn from the fact that the watch-dog fights while the wild dog often runs away. Of the husband, as of the house-dog, it may often be said that he has been tamed into ferocity.

This is especially true of the sort of house represented by the country cottage. It is only in theory that the things are petty and prosaic; a man realistically experiencing them will feel them to be things big and baffling and involving a heavy battle with nature. When we read about cabbages or cauliflowers in the papers, and especially the comic papers, we learn to think of them as commonplace. But if a man of any imagination will merely consent to walk round the kitchen-garden for himself, and really looks at the cabbages and cauliflowers, he will feel at once that they are vast and elemental things like the mountains in the clouds. He will feel something almost monstrous about the size and solidity of the things swelling out of that small and tidy patch of ground. There are moods in which that everyday English kitchen plot will affect him as men are affected by the reeking wealth and toppling rapidity of tropic vegetation; the green bubbles and crawling branches of a nightmare.

But whatever his mood, he will see that things so large and work so laborious cannot possibly be merely trivial. His reason no less than his imagination will tell him that the fight here waged between the family and the field is of all things the most primitive and fundamental. If that is not poetical, nothing is poetical, and certainly not the dingy Bohemianism of the artists in the towns. But the point for the moment is that even by the purely artistic test the same truth is apparent. An artist looking at these things with a free and a fresh vision will at once appreciate what I mean by calling them wild rather than tame. It is true of fire, of water, of vegetation, of half a hundred other things. If a man reads about a pig, he will think of something comic and commonplace, chiefly because the word " pig " sounds comic and commonplace. If he looks at a real pig in a real pigsty, he will have the sense of something too large to be alive, like a hippopotamus at the Zoo.

This is not a coincidence or a sophistry; it rests on the real and living logic of things. The family is itself a wilder thing than the State; if we mean by wildness that it is born of will and choice as elemental and emancipated as the wind. It has its own laws, as the wind has; but properly understood it is infinitely less subservient than things are under the elaborate and mechanical regulations of legalism. Its obligations are love and loyalty, but these are things quite capable of being in revolt against merely human laws; for merely human law has a great tendency to become merely inhuman law. It is concerned with events that are in the moral world what cyclones and earthquakes are in the material world.

People are not born in an infant-school any more than they die in an undertaker's shop. These prodigies are private things; and take place in the tiny theatre of the home. The public systems, the large organisation, are a mere machinery for the transport and distribution of things; they do not touch the intrinsic nature of the things themselves. If a birthday present is sent from one family to another all the legal system, and even all that we call the social system, is only concerned with the present so long as it is a parcel. Nearly all our modern sociology might be called the philosophy of parcels. For that matter, nearly all our modern descriptions of Utopia or the Great State might be called the paradise of postmen. It is in the inner chamber that the parcel becomes a present; that it explodes, so to speak, into its own radiance and real popularity; and it is equally true, so far as that argument is concerned, whether it is a bon-bon or a bomb. The essential message is always a personal message; the important business is always private business. And this is, of course, especially with the first of all birthday presents which presents itself at birth; and it is no exaggeration to talk of a bomb as the symbol of a baby. Of course, the same is true of the tragic as of the beatific acts of the domestic drama; of the spadework of the struggle for life or the Damoclean sword of death.

The defence of domesticity is not that it is always happy, or even that it is always harmless. It is rather that it does involve, like all heroic things, the possibilities of calamity and even of crime. Old Mother Hubbard may find that the cupboard is bare; she may even find a skeleton in the cupboard. All that is involved here is the insistence on the true case for this intimate type of association; that in itself it is certainly not commonplace and most certainly is not conventional. The conventions belong rather to those wider worldly organisations which are now set up as rivals to it; to the club, to the school and above all to the State. You cannot have a successful club without rules; but a family will really do without rules exactly in proportion as it is a successful family. What somebody said about the songs of a people could be said much more truly about the jokes of a household. And a joke is in its nature a wild and spontaneous thing; even the modern fanaticism for organisation has never really attempted to organise laughter like a chorus. Therefore, we may truly say that these external emblems or examples of something grotesque and extravagant about our private possessions are not mere artistic exercises in the incongruous; they are not, as the phrase goes, mere paradoxes. They are really related to the aboriginal nature of the institution itself and the idea that is behind it. The real family is something as wild and elemental as a cabbage.

# THE PHANTOM BUTLER

IN the police news, which is the most respectable and reliable part of a modern newspaper, our eye was recently riveted with astonishment by the following phrase: "So-and-so, described as a butler of no fixed abode." This is what may be called a really revolutionary image. Kings may fall and go wandering in exile; and peasants may be turned into street arabs by the advance of progress and invention; but the thought of a butler with nothing to buttle is deeply disturbing. A butler blown upon the winds; a butler singing in the wilderness; a butler passing through sleeping villages at midnight, complete in his butler's uniform and with his solemn face turned up to the moon, has about it something very creepy and unnatural. Does he build about him in the desert an invisible pantry or go through all the phantom gestures of one drawing corks and receiving tips? Is he heard whispering to the wild flowers at evening: "You will be requiring the sherry, sir," or crying sternly to the morning larks that his lordship is engaged? Does he stop a stranger in the street and become his butler for a few minutes by sheer force of character and presence? Does he assume the butler manner among the tramps in a shelter, and does he emerge alive? However it may be with these mysteries, a butler made quite as mysterious an appearance in a quarrel about Spiritualism which once raged between Sir Arthur Conan Doyle and a sceptic. Sir Arthur said that a certain photograph showed a phantom figure seated in an armchair in a certain library; a figure which he identified with that of a dead lord once associated with the house. We have not seen the photograph but in justice to Sir Arthur's side, we are bound to say that the sceptic's version seems rather more mysterious than the mystic's. Apparently the sceptic began by saying that the ghost of the aristocrat was only an accidental flaw in the photographic plate. Afterwards, by way of an afterthought, he said it was a butler, who had come into the room and sat down without disturbing any of the social arrangements. Now we have seen more than one aristocrat whose face might very well have been a flaw in a photographic plate. We have seen more than one butler whose existence we should be glad to explain by some such operation of accident or disaster, rather than design. But if a splash of chemicals can so easily be turned into a live butler, it seems not altogether unnatural that it should be turned into a dead lord. And it seems rather more probable, in the abstract, that a dead lord would refuse to allow such a trifle as death to prevent him from sitting in his own armchair than that any living butler that we have ever heard of would have so frivolously intruded himself into that position. This butler, at any rate, was not a butler of no fixed abode. He seems to have been a butler who made himself rather too much at home. He carried domesticity almost to excess; and trusted a little too much to the ties of environment.

> In my opinion butlers ought
> To know their place and not to play
> The old retainer night and day.

This was an old retainer whom some would even hesitate to retain. It is possible, by another theory, that it was indeed this singular attendant who suffered some such expulsion, and went wandering through the world with no fixed abode, a figure far more weird than any spectre of any nobleman. On the whole, if we had to choose, we would as soon believe in the ghost as not; so we will for the sake of argument accept the remarkable seance at which the dead lord takes the chair. If Spiritualists do show a great deal of credulity about spirit photographs, sceptics show almost as much credulity about faked photographs. Preternatural explanations seem quite mild and tame compared with the preposterous natural explanations that are given; in which butlers flash and fade on a photographic plate at least as elusively as fairies.

TERRIBLE EFFECT OF XMAS +

Publishers, Editors, Business Men, Middlemen, Lecture Agents & Officials hearing that Miss Collins is on her holiday & come out of their lairs and catch Mr G.K. Chesterton napping.

Publishers, Creditors, Interviewers, Cranks etc — fleeing before the Perfect Secretary.

# THE JOYS OF SCIENCE

I TOOK her and I flattened her
Respectfully, I hope——
I pasted her upon a slip
Under the microscope,
With six-power lens I spied her,
Ah, ne'er shall I forget,
While hearts can beat and flowers bloom,
That hour when first we met.

Oh with what prayers and fasting
Shall mortal man deserve
To see that glimpse of Heaven
Her motor vagus nerve.
Look not, ye too inflammable,
Beneath that harmless hair,
The convolutions of her brain
Are perilously fair.

I breathed into that microscope
A Vow of burning tone,
I swore by men and angels,
The thunder and the throne,
That ere one brave, brown hair were touched
On that triumphant head
My serum's red corpuscula
Should cheerfully be shed.

# THE JOYS OF SCIENCE

Spurn not the men of Science,
They sob beneath your sneers
As with their large thermometers
They test their burning tears,
Because they rend the rock and flower
To prove, is this their sin,
Nature, the good King's daughter,
All glorious within.

Natural annoyance of William Shakespeare on being asked (while engaged on "Macbeth") for the exact time of one of his Sonnets, by a Journalist from Beaconsfield ————

# THE LEGEND OF THE SWORD

A STRANGE story is told of the Spanish-American War, of a sort that sounds like the echo of some older epic; of how an active Yankee, pursuing the enemy, came at last to a forgotten Spanish station on an island and felt as if he had intruded on the presence of a ghost. For he found in a house hung with ragged Cordova leather and old gold tapestries a Spaniard as out of time as Don Quixote, who had no weapon but an ancient sword. This he declared his family had kept bright and sharp since the days of Cortes: and it may be imagined with what a smile the American regarded it, standing spick and span with his Sam Browne belt and his new service revolver.

His amusement was naturally increased when he found, moored close by, the gilded skeleton of an old galley. When the Spanish spectre sprang on board, brandishing his useless weapon, and his captor followed, the whole parted amidships and the two were left clinging to a spar. And here (says the legend) the story took a strange turn: for they floated far on this rude raft together: and were ultimately cast up on a desert island.

The shelving shores of the island were covered with a jungle of rush and tall grasses, which it was necessary to clear away, both to make space for a hut and to plait mats or curtains for it. With an activity rather surprising in one so slow and old-fashioned, the Spaniard drew his sword and began to use it in the manner of a scythe. The other asked if he could assist.

"This, as you say, is a rude and antiquated tool," replied the swordsman, "and your own is a weapon of precision and promptitude. If, therefore, you (with your unerring aim) will condescend to shoot off each blade of grass, one at a time, who can doubt that the task will be more rapidly accomplished?"

The face of the Iberian, under the closest scrutiny, seemed full of gravity and even gloom: and the work continued in silence. In spite of his earthy toils, however, the Hidalgo contrived to remain reasonably neat and spruce: and the puzzle was partially solved one morning when the American, rising early, found his comrade shaving himself with the sword, which that foolish family legend had kept particularly keen.

"A man with no earthly possessions but an old iron blade," said the Spaniard apologetically, "must shave himself as best he can. But you, equipped as you are with every luxury of science, will have no difficulty in shooting off your whiskers with a pistol."

So far from profiting by this graceful felicitation, the modern traveller seemed for a moment a little ruffled or put out: then he said abruptly, unslinging his revolver, "Well, I guess I can't eat my whiskers, anyhow; and this little toy may be more use in getting breakfast."

And blazing away rapidly and with admirable aim, he brought down five birds and emptied his revolver.

"Let me assure you," said the other courteously, "that you have provided the materials for more than one elegant repast. Only after that, your ammunition being now exhausted, shall we have to fall back on a clumsy trick of mine, of spiking fish on the sword."

" You can spike me now, I suppose, as well as the fish," said the other bitterly. " We seem to have sunk back into a state of barbarism."

" We have sunk into a state," said the Spaniard, nodding gravely, " in which we can get anything we want with what we have got already."

" But," cried the American, " that is the end of all Progress ! "

" I wonder whether it matters much which end ? " said the other.

# PLAKKOPYTRIXOPHYLISPERAMBULANTIOBATRIX

*(A Twenty Minutes' Holiday from Writing Fiction.* 12 *p.m.)*

FEAR not, fear not, my children,
The last weird embers fade,
Blue corpses through the windows peer,
But still you seem afraid,
Perhaps there's Something in the room,
Whatever would you do
If I were not among you now
To cheer and comfort you?

Heed not that pale thing in the door,
It smiles so like a skull,
You hear hoarse spectres scream and clank,
You find the evening dull?
Then let me tell a merry tale
Of dear old days of yore,
About a dragon of the wastes
That drank of human gore.

It dwelt among untrodden ways,
And ate the plaintive dove;
A dragon there were few to praise
And very few to love.

## PLAKKOPYTRIXOPHYLISPERAMBULANTIOBATRIX

(I use this piece of Wordsworth
To show how much I know)
Uproariously popular
It was, as dragons go.

If I could only paint the Thing!
Just imitate its wink,
All you five infants, one by one,
Would rise and take to drink:
Or roll in death-pangs on the floor,
And lie there choked and blue,
O how I wish I could describe
This animal to you.

Some swore its fur was bushy brown,
Some swore that it was green,
With savage eyes of bluish grey:
Some swore that they had seen
In coils upon a sofa wreathed,
It, writhing as in pangs,
And tearing Bovril chocolate
With huge, abhorrent fangs.

Some said that far to eastward
They saw It, garbed in grey,
Standing upon a platform
And bellowing all day.
Some said that far to northward,
Through all the white snow-wreath,
They saw it, white and wolfish,
With half-a-million teeth.

# PLAKKOPYTRIXOPHYLISPERAMBULANTIOBATRIX

When skies were blue with summer
It glittered, bright and blue,
And once, the stricken wanderer
In screaming terror flew,
For on the shining tableland
White gauze did round it glance,
And with one rose to crown it
He saw the dragon dance.

The Witless Youth in wonder
Sat lank upon a stone,
His Hat was monumental
Its secret—all his own.
The Sage was mild and hoary
And skilled in Wisdom's page,
The Youth sat meek (as always)
And to him spoke the Sage.

" Go not to smite the Dragon
That wasteth field and fen,
Around her reeking cavern
Are strewn the hearts of men;
But youth is foolish: You, Sir,
Are singularly so—
So learn her horrid habits
At least, before you go.

" If you would raise her bristles up
And set her eye in flames,
Then seek the Hankin-Pankin
And read the Jenry-James;

## PLAKKOPYTRIXOPHYLISPERAMBULANTIOBATRIX

Go with a train of spiders huge
With all their threads and thrums
From ledgers all declaiming
Interminable sums . . .

" But would you see the awful smile,
And soften down the Eye,
Then fetch the Stompy-Steinthal
And bring the Rompy-Rye;
And choirs of ladies tall and proud
With all one kind of nose,
And bucketsful of flowers
And basketsful of clothes."

*(Unfinished, or if finished the last page has been lost.)*

Just Indignation of Queen Victoria —→

# CHRISTMAS AND THE FIRST GAMES

I HAVE sometimes been haunted with a vague story about a wild and fantastic uncle, the enemy of parents and the cause of revolution in nurseries, who went about preaching a certain theory; I mean the theory that all the objects which children use at Christmas for what we call riotous or illegitimate purposes, were originally created for those purposes; and not for the humdrum household purposes which they now serve. For instance, we will suppose that the story begins with a pillow-fight in a night-nursery; and boys buffeting and bashing each other with those white and shapeless clubs. The uncle, who would be a professor of immense learning and even greater imagination and inventiveness, would proceed to make himself unpopular with parents and popular with children, by proving that the pillow in prehistoric art is obviously designed to be a club; that the sham-fight in the night-nursery is actually more ancient and authoritative than the whole institution of beds or bedclothes; that in some innocent morning of the world such cherubim warred on each other with such clouds, possibly made of white samite, mystic, wonderful, and stuffed with feathers from the angels' wings; and that it was only afterwards, when weariness fell upon the world and the young gods had grown tired of their godlike sports, that they slept with their heads upon their weapons; and so, by a gradual dislocation of the whole original purpose of the pillow, it came to be recognised as having its proper place on a bed. It is obvious that any number of these legends could be launched with ease and grace and general gratification.

It would be urged, to eagerly assenting little boys, that catapults are really older and more majestic than windows. Windows were merely targets set up for catapults, clear and fragile that such archaic archers might be rewarded with a crash and sparkle of crystal; that it was only after the oppressive priesthood of the Middle Paleolithic had ruthlessly suppressed the Catapult Culture, that people had gradually come to use the now useless glass targets for purposes of light or ventilation. Similarly, butter was originally used solely to make butter-slides in the path of parents and guardians and it was only by a late accident in the life of some prominent though prostrate citizen, who happened to lick the pavement, that its edible qualities were discovered, like the edible qualities of roast pork in Charles Lamb's story. The subversive principle can be applied to almost every childish game; it may be said that primitive hunters hunted the slipper, long before that leaping and elusive animal was duplicated and worn as furry spoils upon the feet of the hunter. It might be said that no handkerchief was ever used to blow the nose, as in our degenerate day, till it had been used for centuries to blind the eyes, as in the hierarchic mystery of Blind-Man's-Buff.

True, I cannot set forth here in any great detail any actual proofs of these prehistoric origins; but I never heard of anybody bothering about historic proofs in connection with prehistoric origins. There is quite as much evidence for my favourite uncle's theory of the primitive pillow as there is for Mr. H. G. Wells's detailed account of the horrible Old Man, who ruled by terror over twenty or thirty younger men who could have thrown him out of the cave on his ape-like ear; there is as much scientific proof as there is for Dr. Freud's highly modern and morbid romance about a whole race of sexual perverts making a whole religious service out of parricide; there is as much in the way of data for demonstration as in Mr. Gerald Heard's sentimental film-scenario about arboreal anthropoids kissing the stones which they throw at lions. Nobody expects any historic evidence for things of this sort, because they are prehistoric; and nobody dreams of attempting to found them on any scientific facts; they are simply Science. I do not see why my favourite uncle and I should not be Science too. I do not see why we should not simply make things up out of our own heads; things which cannot possibly be contradicted, just as they cannot possibly be proved. The only difference is that my uncle and I, especially when we set out with a general intention of talking about Christmas, cannot manage to work up that curious loathing of the human race, which is now considered essential to any history written for humanitarians. Dr. Freud (as is perhaps natural after a heavy day of psychopathic interviews) seems to have taken quite a dislike to human beings. So when he makes up the story of how their first forgotten institutions arose in utterly unrecorded times, he makes the family story as nasty as he can; like any other modern novelist. But my uncle and I (especially at Christmas) happen to feel in a more cheerful and charitable frame of mind; and, as there are no iron creeds or dogmas to restrain anybody from anything, we have as much right to imagine cheerful things as he has to imagine gloomy ones. And we beg to announce, with the same authority, that everything began with a celestial pillow-fight of cherubs, or that the whole world was made entirely for the games of children.

The two or three truths, of which my uncle's hypothesis is at least symbolic or suggestive, may be conveniently arranged thus. First, it must always be remembered that there really is a mystery, and something resembling a religious mystery, in the origin of many things which have since become (very rightly) practical and (very wrongly) prosaic. If my uncle in a festive moment declared that fireworks came before fires, and were used to blazon the blackness of night with ceremonial illuminations, before it was even noticed that they could cook our food or warm our hands, he might not be speaking with pedantic precision; but he would not be far off from a considerable historical truth. There are many strange traces of the ritual side of tilling or tending animals preceding the practical side. Second, it must be remembered that these rituals, including Christmas, have been on the whole preserved most continuously by the populace; for a true populace is far more traditional than an aristocracy. They have been preserved by poor people, though generally by poor people who possessed some small property; in short, most markedly by a peasantry. Thus, if my uncle, rising hilariously once more, were to propound to the company the opinion that the Christmas stocking stuffed with gifts and strung onto the bedpost, was a thing far more ancient and authoritative than mere common human stockings as degraded to be the livery of common human legs, I should soothe him by assuring him that I saw his point, though I might not accept this literal illustration of it.

Now it is very interesting to remember that there is another proverb, or traditional truth, about stockings in connection with peasants. It has often been said that the peasant put his small property into his stocking, stuck his little hoard of gold into his stocking, so that it might be safe from thieves and bankers. And the peasant was lectured to about this, by no less than nine thousand, nine hundred and ninety-nine lecturers on political economy and professional professors of economics or high finance. It was patiently pointed out to him that metal coins do not breed like maggots when left in a stocking; that guineas do not have little families of guineas as guinea-pigs do of guinea-pigs; that a stocking is not a nest in which a sovereign can lay half-sovereigns as a bird lays eggs; or, in more learned but less sensible language, that his money was not bringing him in any interest. So that the only way to make money do what money cannot do, and the only true scientific scheme for proving there is a guinea-and-a-half when there is only a guinea, is to put it in a bank. A bank, as the nine thousand professors of economics explained to the stupid or stupefied peasant can never fail to pay interest. A stocking may wear out or have holes in it; thieves may break in and steal; but it is manifestly impossible for bankers to steal; and even a violation of nature's laws for things in banks to be stolen; much more for them to disappear altogether, in so brisk and busy a centre of speculation. Since banks cannot conceivably fail, argued the professors, you would obviously be a richer man, with somebody else's money from somewhere somehow mysteriously added to your own, if you would take it out of the stocking and put it into the bank. The peasant was still dazed; but he was strangely stubborn. Since then, the situation has been modified in various ways; and a good many of the professors are wishing they had imitated the peasant.

# Signs of the Last Days: ———.

Embarrassment of a Clergyman at having to separate
a sheep from the goats. ——

# A BALLADE OF A STOIC

THE griefs of friends how grave they often are!
They've smashed my friend's five Titians in their frames.
My cousin broke three ribs beneath a car
And had to pay for it in counter-claims;
My mother's favourite chapel is in flames;
My father's best cashier is going blind;
My niece is mad; my nephew's name is James;
My aunt is murdered—and I do not mind.

O cell where Socrates was like a star!
O soul of Cato that no death defames!
The field where Montfort fell with many a scar;
The gallows of the noblest of the Graemes;
All these my larger virtue lops and lames
I am the Hero by the gods designed,
The Stoic whom no lash of fortune tames.
My aunt is murdered—and I do not mind.

I had no hand in this distressing spar.
When the assassin told me of his aims
I handed him a heavy iron bar
And turned my back and watched the widening Thames.
It's no good blaming me or calling names.
The Age of Chivalry is left behind;
I don't profess to be a Squire of Dames.
My aunt is murdered—and I do not mind.

# A BALLADE OF A STOIC

## Envoi

Prince, what—in tears?  Oh sight that shocks and shames!
Because the fifteenth housemaid has resigned,
Come let us play those nice expensive games.
My aunt is murdered; and *I* do not mind.

# A NIGHTMARE

In the dimly lighted railway carriage a man had been talking to me about the structural weakness of St. Paul's Cathedral. He spoke in a bold, fresh, scientific spirit, and I suppose I had gone to sleep. At any rate, when I roused myself at Blackfriars Station and found myself alone I felt unusually chilly, and the station seemed unusually dark. I dropped on the dim platform, however, and went quickly across it, with the swinging rapidity of a routine, to the exit where stood the ticket-collector. He was not dressed like a ticket-collector, however. For some reason (possibly the cold I had myself remarked) he was cloaked from head to foot in a black hooded gown, such as had been worn centuries before by those friars after whom the place was named. And instead of taking my ticket he only said to me, " Do not go upstairs."

I looked at him with a dull wonder, and then I looked around equally doubtfully. It seemed to me that other monkish forms had gathered in the shadows, and that the place was like a monastery, with every light extinguished.

" Do not go upstairs," said the hooded man. " You will not like what is being done there. A man like you had far better stay with us."

" Do you calmly propose," I asked, " that I should stay in the Underground for ever? "

" Yes, in the Underground," he answered. " We of the ancient Church remained in the Underground, in the Catacombs. For what was done in the daylight was not good for a good man to see."

"What on earth is it?" I asked. "Is there a massacre?"

"Would to God," he answered, "that it were only that!"

"I will go up!" I cried. "It is open air, at any rate."

"Consider it well," he answered, with curious calm. "We guard ourselves with walls; we gird ourselves with sackcloth. But our laughter and our levity are within. But the new philosophers are girt all round with gaiety, and their despair is in their hearts."

"I will go up," I cried, and broke past him and ran upstairs.

Yet I did it with such swollen and expectant passions that I took it for granted that I should rush out upon some enormous orgy, obvious and obscene in the sunlight. And it was like the first crash into cold water when I found myself in an utterly empty street, turned almost white by the moon.

I strode up the street, turned two corners, and stood before St. Paul's Cathedral. It stood up quite cold and colossal in the empty night, like the lost temple of some empty planet. Only, when I had stared a little while, I saw the foolish figure of a young man standing straddling on the uppermost steps, as if he owned the Cathedral.

The instant I had started to mount the steps he waved at me wildly and cried, "Have you got a new design?"

And as I paused irresolute there popped like rabbits out of their holes, three pale men from between the pillars, peering at me.

The young man ran half-way down the steps, and I saw that he had long wandering auburn hair and an impudent smile, but his face was whiter than a corpse's.

"We have cleared the London streets," he explained, "of everyone who has not a design. These three gentlemen have all got new designs. That one," he added, lowering his voice and pointing at one man, who had a hairless head and huge ears, " That one is Pyffer himself."

" And who is Pyffer?" I asked, staring at the man, whose horrible ears seemed to grow larger as I stared.

" You know the great pessimist, surely," he asked anxiously. " But you must not speak to him. He never speaks. He sometimes—seems to begin to speak, but it always ends in a yawn. Yet how well that yawn seems to express his terrible creed!"

I had reached the top step, and now saw the other two men more clearly: one was a blonde German with watery eyes and wild moustaches. The other was an elderly man with black whiskers and green spectacles. He was in the middle of an oration when I reached him.

" It is merely," he said, "a matter of science—a matter for experts. What could be more absurd than the present construction of the thing?"

At this point the pale young man (who seemed to be a sort of showman) whispered in my ear: " Dr. Blood; he has made Conduct a science."

Dr. Blood continued: " What can be more absurd, architecturally, than that singular object at the top of the cathedral; I mean the object with the projecting arms? Think of putting up a thing with projecting arms, and expecting it to stand upright? The ball, too, is obviously top-heavy. The dome is a curve. I am against curves."

He paused for an instant, and Professor Pyffer opened his mouth as if to speak. Then he opened his mouth as if to shout; and then he shut in silence. He had only yawned.

" In that yawn," whispered the young man to me, " he has swallowed all the stars."

I replied that they did not seem to agree with him; but Dr. Blood was still going on.

" The matter is to an expert, obvious. The thing at the top should be a small cube of stone. The ball should be a cube of stone slightly larger. The dome should be represented by a cube larger still, and so on. If it were built like that, it would never fall down."

" Has it ever occurred to you," I asked, " that if it were built like that we should want it to fall down? "

" The stranger speaks right," broke in the fair man with the watery eyes. " It should be upwards ever! From the man to the superman! From the structure to the superstructure! I will tell you the fault of your architecture; it is not upon the nature-energy based! Your churches are larger at the bottom, smaller at the top. But the all-mother-born trees are smaller at the bottom, larger at the top. So should this cathedral be. In the first floor two domes, in the second floor three domes, in the third floor, and so on, ever branching, ever increasing, each landing larger than the last one, till at last . . . "

He had flung up his arms in a rigid ecstasy. His voice failed, but his arms remained vertical; so we all murmured " Quite so."

Then Dr. Blood said in a curious, cool voice, " Now you trust the expert. I'll put this place right in two minutes."

He strode into the interior, and then we heard three taps. And the next moment this dome that filled the sky shook as in an earthquake, and tilted sideways. Nothing could express the enormous unreason of that familiar scene silently gone wrong.

I awoke to hear the hoarse voice of the yawning man, speaking for the first and last time in my ear.

" Do you see," he whispered, " the sky is crooked? "

THREE ACRES
and a Cow.

# HOMESICK AT HOME

ONE, seeming to be a traveller, came to me and said, "What is the shortest journey from one place to the same place?"

The sun was behind his head, so that his face was illegible.

"Surely," I said, "to stand still."

"That is no journey at all," he replied. "The shortest journey from one place to the same place is round the world." And he was gone.

White Wynd had been born, brought up, married and made the father of a family in the White Farmhouse by the river. The river enclosed it on three sides like a castle: on the fourth side there were stables and beyond that a kitchen-garden and beyond that an orchard and beyond that a low wall and beyond that a road and beyond that a pinewood and beyond that a cornfield and beyond that slopes meeting the sky, and beyond that—but we must not catalogue the whole earth, though it is a great temptation. White Wynd had known no other home but this. Its walls were the world to him and its roof the sky.

This is what makes his action so strange.

In his later years he hardly ever went outside the door. And as he grew lazy he grew restless: angry with himself and everyone. He found himself in some strange way weary of every moment and hungry for the next.

His heart had grown stale and bitter towards the wife and children whom he saw every day, though they were five of the good faces of the earth. He remembered, in glimpses, the days of his toil and strife for bread, when, as he came home in the evening, the thatch of his home burned with gold as though angels were standing there. But he remembered it as one remembers a dream.

Now he seemed to be able to see other homes, but not his own. That was merely a house. Prose had got hold of him: the sealing of the eyes and the closing of the ears.

At last something occurred in his heart: a volcano; an earthquake; an eclipse; a daybreak; a deluge; an apocalypse. We might pile up colossal words, but we should never reach it.

Eight hundred times the white daylight had broken across the bare kitchen as the little family sat at breakfast. And the eight hundred and first time the father paused with the cup he was passing in his hand.

" That green cornfield through the window," he said dreamily, " shining in the sun. Somehow, somehow it reminds me of a field outside my own home."

" Your own home? " cried his wife. " This is your home."

White Wynd rose to his feet, seeming to fill the room. He stretched forth his hand and took a staff. He stretched it forth again and took a hat. The dust came in clouds from both of them.

" Father," cried one child. " Where are you going? "

" Home," he replied.

" What can you mean? This is your home. What home are you going to? "

" To the White Farmhouse by the river."

" This is it."

He was looking at them very tranquilly when his eldest daughter caught sight of his face.

" Oh, he is mad ! " she screamed, and buried her face in her hands.

He spoke calmly. " You are a little like my eldest daughter," he said. " But you haven't got the look, no, not the look which is a welcome after work."

" Madam," he said, turning to his thunderstruck wife with a stately courtesy. " I thank you for your hospitality, but indeed I fear I have trespassed on it too long. And my home——"

" Father, father, answer me ! Is not this your home ? "

The old man waved his stick.

" The rafters are cobwebbed, the walls are rain-stained. The doors bind me, the rafters crush me. There are littlenesses and bickerings and heartburnings here behind the dusty lattices where I have dozed too long. But the fire roars and the door stands open. There is bread and raiment, fire and water and all the crafts and mysteries of love. There is rest for heavy feet on the matted floor, and for starved heart in the pure faces, far away at the end of the world, in the house where I was born."

" Where, where ? "

" In the White Farmhouse by the river."

And he passed out of the front door, the sun shining on his face.

And the other inhabitants of the White Farmhouse stood staring at each other.

White Wynd was standing on the timber bridge across the river, with the world at his feet.

And a great wind came flying from the opposite edge of the sky (a land of marvellous pale golds) and met him. Some may know what that first wind outside the door is to a man. To this man it seemed that God had bent back his head by the hair and kissed him on the forehead.

He had been weary with resting, without knowing that the whole remedy lay in sun and wind and his own body. Now he half believed that he wore the seven-leagued boots.

He was going home. The White Farmhouse was behind every wood and beyond every mountain wall. He looked for it as we all look for fairyland, at every turn of the road. Only in one direction he never looked for it, and that was where, only a thousand yards behind him, the White Farmhouse stood up, gleaming with thatch and whitewash against the gusty blue of morning.

He looked at the dandelions and crickets and realised that he was gigantic. We are too fond of reckoning always by mountains. Every object is infinitely vast as well as infinitely small.

He stretched himself like one crucified in an uncontainable greatness.

" Oh God, who hast made me and all things, hear four songs of praise. One for my feet that Thou hast made strong and light upon Thy daisies. One for my head, which Thou hast lifted and crowned above the four corners of Thy heaven. One for my heart, which Thou hast made a heaven of angels singing Thy glory. And one for that pearl-tinted cloudlet far away above the stone pines on the hill."

He felt like Adam newly created. He had suddenly inherited all things, even the suns and stars.

Have you ever been out for a walk?

The story of the journey of White Wynd would be an epic. He was swallowed up in huge cities and forgotten: yet he came out on the other side. He worked in quarries, and in docks in country after country. Like a transmigrating soul, he lived a series of existences: a knot of vagabonds, a colony of workmen, a crew of sailors, a group of fishermen, each counted him a final fact in their lives, the great spare man with eyes like two stars, the stars of an ancient purpose.

But he never diverged from the line that girdles the globe.

On a mellow summer evening, however, he came upon the strangest thing in all his travels. He was plodding up a great dim down, that hid everything, like the dome of the earth itself.

Suddenly a strange feeling came over him. He glanced back at the waste of turf to see if there were any trace of boundary, for he felt like one who has just crossed the border of elfland. With his head a belfry of new passions, assailed with confounding memories, he toiled on the brow of the slope.

The setting sun was raying out a universal glory. Between him and it, lying low on the fields, there was what seemed to his swimming eyes a white cloud. No, it was a marble palace. No, it was the White Farmhouse by the river.

He had come to the end of the world. Every spot on earth is either the beginning or the end, according to the heart of man. That is the advantage of living on an oblate spheroid.

It was evening. The whole swell of turf on which he stood was turned to gold. He seemed standing in fire instead of grass. He stood so still that the birds settled on his staff.

All the earth and the glory of it seemed to rejoice round the madman's homecoming. The birds on their way to their nests knew him, Nature herself was in his secret, the man who had gone from one place to the same place.

But he leaned wearily on his staff. Then he raised his voice once more.

" O God, who hast made me and all things, hear four songs

231

of praise. One for my feet, because they are sore and slow, now that they draw near the door. One for my head, because it is bowed and hoary, now that Thou crownest it with the sun. One for my heart, because Thou hast taught it in sorrow and hope deferred that it is the road that makes the home. And one for that daisy at my feet."

He came down over the hillside and into the pinewood. Through the trees he could see the red and gold sunset settling down among the white farm-buildings and the green apple-branches. It was his home now. But it could not be his home till he had gone out from it and returned to it. Now he was the Prodigal Son.

He came out of the pinewood and across the road. He surmounted the low wall and tramped through the orchard, through the kitchen garden, past the cattle-sheds. And in the stony courtyard he saw his wife drawing water.

# AFTERWORD

If Gilbert Chesterton is one of your heroes, as he is one of mine, you'll find this anthology crammed with some of G.K.'s delightful youthful writings. The book was put together by Maisie Ward in 1938, two years after Chesterton's death. Miss Ward was G.K.'s friend, and adviser. Some dozen lives of Chesterton have since been written, none better or more accurate than Miss Ward's 685-page *Gilbert Keith Chesterton*.

The book you now hold is the only book that reproduces in dazzling color a raft of Chesterton's early art, as well as eight amusing uncolored self-caricatures.

*The Coloured Lands,* a short story published here for the first time, is about a strange young man who lets a boy named Tommy look through four spectacles made with colored glass that turn everything into blue, red, yellow, or green. The man tells Tommy that when he was a child he had been fascinated by colored glasses, but soon tired of seeing the world in single colors. In a rose-red city, he explains, you can't see the color of a rose because everything is red. At the suggestion of a powerful wizard, the man was told to paint the scenery any way he liked:

> "So I set to work very carefully; first blocking in a great deal of blue, because I thought it would throw up a sort of square of white in the middle; and then I thought a fringe of a sort of dead gold would look well along the top of the white; and I spilt some green at the bottom of

233

it. As for red, I had already found out the secret about red. You have to have a very little of it to make a lot of it. So I just made a row of little blobs of bright red on the white just above the green; and as I went on working at the details, I slowly discovered what I was doing; which is what very few people ever discover in this world. I found I had put back, bit by bit, the whole of that picture over there in front of us. I had made that white cottage with the thatch and that summer sky behind it and that green lawn below; and the row of the red flowers just as you see them now. That is how they come to be there. I thought you might be interested to know it."

As far as I know, Chesterton never read any of L. Frank Baum's fourteen Oz books. Had he done so, I believe he would have been entranced to learn that each of the five regions of Oz is dominated by a single color. Munchkin land is blue, the Winkie region is yellow, the southern Quadling country is red, the northern Gillikin region purple, and of course the Emerald City is green. Chesterton was fond of every color. One of his best essays, "The Glory of Gray," praises gray for its power as background to intensify colors.

In her fine Introduction to *The Coloured Lands,* Maisie Ward reminds us of what G.K. called the "central idea" of his life—that we should all learn to see everything, from a sunflower to the cosmos, as a miracle, and to be perpetually thankful for the privilege of being alive. Would things not be much simpler and easier to comprehend if nothing existed? This sense of awe toward the terrible mystery of why there is something rather than nothing—of why, as Stephen Hawking once wrote, the universe "bothers to exist"—can arouse an emotion so close to what Sartre called nausea, and William James called a metaphysical wonder sickness, that if it lasted more than a few moments we could go mad. In *The Coloured Lands* this emotion comes through strongly in two chapters, one an essay on "Wonder and the Wooden Post," the other a short story titled "Homesick at Home."Here is a passage from "Wonder and the Wooden Post":

> "When the modern mystics said they liked to see a post, they meant they liked to imagine it. They were better poets than I; and they imagined it as soon as they saw it. Now I might see a post long before I had imagined it—and (as I have already described) I might feel it before I saw it. To me the post is wonderful because it is there; there whether I like it or not. I was struck silly by a post, but if I were struck blind by a thunderbolt, the post would still be there; the substance of things not seen. For the amazing thing about the universe is that it exists; not that we can discuss its existence. All real spirituality is a testimony to this world as much as the other: the material universe does exist. The Cosmos still quivers to its topmost star from that great kick that Dr. Johnson gave the stone when he defied Berkeley. The kick was not philosophy—but it was religion.

"Homesick at Home" anticipates Chesterton's long forgotten novel *Manalive,* in print as a Dover paperback (0-486-41405-1). In this short story a man with the unlikely name of White Wynd sets out on a trip around the world so he can return to recapture a fading sense of wonder and gratitude for his wife and home. In *Manalive,* one of G.K.'s funniest fantasies, White Wynd is replaced by Innocent Smith who circumnavigates the globe for the same reason

# AFTERWORD

Wynd did. I urge you to read this curious novel. You'll find a chapter about it in my book, *The Fantastic Fiction of Gilbert Chesterton*.

One of G.K.'s finest poems, "A Second Childhood," concerns his celebrated sense of wonder toward a universe that to an atheist is what Chesterton called, in an essay on Shelley, "the most exquisite masterpiece ever constructed by nobody." I think it is one of the greatest religious poems ever written. Allow me to quote it in full:

When all my days are ending
And I have no song to sing,
I think I shall not be too old
To stare at everything;
As I stared once at a nursery door
Or a tall tree and a swing.

Wherein God's ponderous mercy hangs
On all my sins and me,
Because He does not take away
The terror from the tree
And stones still shine along the road
That are and cannot be.

Men grow too old for love, my love,
Men grow too old for wine,
But I shall not grow too old to see
Unearthly daylight shine,
Changing my chamber's dust to snow
Till I doubt if it be mine.

Behold, the crowning mercies melt,
The first surprises stay;
And in my dross is dropped a gift
For which I dare not pray:
That a man grow used to grief and joy

But not to night and day.

# AFTERWORD

Men grow too old for love, my love,
Men grow too old for lies,
But I shall not grow too old to see
Enormous night arise.
A cloud that is larger than the world
And a monster made of eyes.

Nor am I worthy to unloose
The latchet of my shoe;
Or shake the dust from off my feet
Or the staff that bears me through
On ground that is too good to last,
Too solid to be true.

Men grow too old for woo, my love,
Men grow too old to wed:
But I shall not grow too old to see
Hung crazily overhead
Incredible rafters when I wake
And find I am not dead.

A thrill of thunder in my hair:
Though blackening clouds be plain,
Still I am stung and startled
By the first drop of the rain:
Romance and pride and passion pass
And these are what remain.

Strange crawling carpets of the grass,
Wide windows of the sky:
So in this perilous grace of God
With all my sins go I:
And things grow new though I grow old,
Though I grow old and die.

MARTIN GARDNER